"So, you've forgiven me?" Mitch asked. "Tell me, Justine."

"Oh, Mitch," she began. He melted at the sound of his name on her lips. "It's not that easy, don't you see? We've had two years stolen, we'll never get them back."

"But are you going to try and tell me you don't want me?" he asked. "That you don't feel anything for me at all?"

She opened her mouth to speak, but he warned her quietly, "Careful, Jussie. You're a rotten liar. And I know exactly how you responded to me earlier—and it wasn't with indifference!"

"It's not that simple," she began uncertainly.

"No, making love isn't simple."

"It wasn't love—"

"Think again," he snapped back furiously.

"Whatever it was, it was a mistake, and we can't do it again," Justine said.

"You have to tell yourself that I'm lying, so you don't have to let go of your anger," Mitch said. "Tell me, Jussie, why would I give up my perfect life to run away when I could have had you? And if I was happy being gone, why would I come back?"

WHAT ARE *LOVESWEPT* ROMANCES?

They are stories of true romance and touching emotion. We believe those two very important ingredients are constants in our highly sensual and very believable stories in the LOVE-SWEPT line. Our goal is to give you, the reader, stories of consistently high quality that may sometimes make you laugh, sometimes make you cry, but are always fresh and creative and contain many delightful surprises within their pages.

Most romance fans read an enormous number of books. Those they truly love, they keep. Others may be traded with friends and soon forgotten. We hope that each LOVESWEPT romance will be a treasure—a "keeper." We will always try to publish

LOVE STORIES YOU'LL NEVER FORGET
BY AUTHORS YOU'LL ALWAYS REMEMBER

The Editors

Loveswept® 900

LOVER COME BACK

JILL SHALVIS

BANTAM BOOKS
NEW YORK · TORONTO · LONDON · SYDNEY · AUCKLAND

LOVER COME BACK
A Bantam Book / August 1998

ISBN 0-553-44646-0

Published simultaneously in the United States and Canada

*Bantam Books are published by Bantam Books, a division of Bantam Dou-
bleday Dell Publishing Group, Inc. Its trademark, consisting of the words
"Bantam Books" and the portrayal of a rooster, is Registered in U.S.
Patent and Trademark Office and in other countries. Marca Registrada.
Bantam Books, 1540 Broadway, New York, New York 10036.*

PRINTED IN THE UNITED STATES OF AMERICA

OPM   10 9 8 7 6 5 4 3 2 1

To DM Jean—for the kid talk, the book talk, the man talk. For the cookies and milk. For always being there. For being my soul sister through thick and thin. Hugs and love always.

ONE

If one more overdressed, intoxicated, holly-jolly male patted her cheek, or any other part of her anatomy, Justine Miller was going to scream. In fact, if anything else went wrong today, she'd explode.

Any normal person who had just gone through what she had would feel this way, she reassured herself. She forced yet another smile and moved through the boisterous Christmas-party crowd, skirting around the huge tree that twinkled merrily with lights. No, she corrected grimly, any "normal" person would have broken down by now and cried. But Justine didn't break down or cry easily, and she wasn't about to start.

"Sis."

Her already tense body tightened as the need to escape nearly overwhelmed her. The grip she had on a still full glass of champagne became perilous. But she'd never run from a problem. *Never*. Besides, this was her beloved brother. He hadn't meant to hurt her. Slowly she turned to face the tall young man with the too-serious blue eyes that matched her own. "Devlin."

"Hi." His nervous gaze swept over her and his mouth fell open. "You look great."

Justine gave him a long look.

He dipped his head, his light red hair falling in his face as he gave her another once-over. "No, I mean it. I haven't seen you in a dress since your wedding two years ago—" He broke off guiltily at her drop-dead glare. "Ah, well . . . It's been a long time. You look . . . different."

"Different?"

"Fine, all right? You look fine."

"Gee, thanks."

"No," he said, smiling. "I'm serious. I never realized your legs were so long, for such a short thing. And I haven't seen your hair down since—"

"Oh, stop it." But she patted her long, dark strawberry-blonde hair self-consciously.

"You should see Mr. Rolland over there. He just keeps looking at you and saying 'wow' over and over again."

"The postmaster is seventy years old, Dev."

He shrugged and grinned. "So? Take it as a compliment."

"Thanks," she said dryly, squelching the urge to smooth down the impossibly short, snug gold scrap that masqueraded as her evening gown. "I think."

She wished she hadn't taken the flute of champagne, but she'd needed something in her nervous hands. She wished she hadn't worn such ridiculously high heels. Mostly, she wished she hadn't accepted the invitation to Mitzy's annual holiday bash. The entire town of Heather

Bay had come, which, in a town as small and cozy as this, wasn't saying much. But still, Justine felt the weight of most of their curious stares, and wondered how long it would take for the gossip to die down this time.

"Devlin, let's go home."

"We can't. You know that. It's important we make an appearance." But he shifted uncomfortably in his suit and Justine narrowed her eyes on him.

She'd raised him. Nearly six years older than he, she knew him well enough to know he was hiding something, and it made her stomach sink like an anchor. "What is it?"

Again he shifted, then lifted an anguished gaze to hers. "Isn't it enough I ruined us? Caused you public humiliation? You need more?"

"All you did was invest unwisely," she said kindly, reaching for his hand. "We'll survive." They always had. "It happens."

"What happened," he said tightly, "is that my stupidity bankrupted us. Got our house taken away. Not to mention having to sell the paper Dad was so proud of, that you worked so hard to run."

She'd managed the *Daily News* despite a mountain of obstacles, including a city full of male chauvinists who still belonged to the old school that said only a man was capable of being editor in chief.

She loved the paper, but loved her brother more. "It's going to be okay."

"There's going to be trouble."

"What's new?" She laughed a little and shrugged. "Trouble's our middle name."

"I brought you into the dreaded limelight. Again." He looked miserable.

"The gossip train would have found something if this hadn't come along," she said gently, sick at how much he hurt too. She tried not to think about the paper that was her life. She'd started there as a teenager, answering phones for ads. Family business or not, she'd had to work her way up, with the help of her journalism degree, all the way to editor in chief. It was just a small daily in a small town, yet she loved it.

But now she had a new boss—that is, if that person intended to keep her as editor. "You still haven't told me who bought us out. I think it's time I meet whomever I'll be working for."

The sudden drain of color from Devlin's face looked all the more noticeable beneath his fair skin. He whispered her name roughly.

The single sip of champagne Justine sampled sizzled flatly in her stomach. Lack of food and frazzled nerves made her dizzy. "Devlin," she said as evenly as she could manage. "What haven't you told me?"

He glanced at the fine crystal she held as if he wished it were his own, filled with straight whiskey.

"Dev," she said, glancing around to make sure they couldn't be heard. No one in the noisy ballroom was close enough. "You're scaring me."

"Justine." Emotion thickened his voice. "I didn't want to hurt you. You've got to remember that. You've been so strong—"

The festive Christmas music in the background blended with the laughter and happy voices, but the holiday spirit had yet to penetrate Justine. Actually, she hadn't felt the holiday spirit in two years. "Just tell me."

Something behind her caught his immediate attention, and he made a strangled sound of regret deep in his throat. A quick glance over her shoulder had her groaning. Mitzy, the mayor's daughter and the apple of the town's eye, hurried toward them, a wide, knowing grin firmly in place. She sparkled as brightly as the lit Christmas tree in her red-sequined dress and flashy earrings. And given the speed at which she moved, she had news. As the society reporter for the paper, she was the center of the social scene in Heather Bay. That, combined with the political ties of her father, made Mitzy one powerful young woman. As a result, she *always* had news, just not the hard kind Justine preferred.

"Justine," Devlin said frantically. "I've got to tell you—"

"Darling," Mitzy said upon reaching them. Smiling coyly from beneath her lashes, she winked at Devlin, whom she'd been trying to coax into her bed since the day she'd turned eighteen. "You look good enough to eat."

"Mitzy, I'm trying to talk to Justine in private—"

"I'm sure you are." She laughed, bringing a perfectly manicured hand to her chest. "But I'm surprised she's still talking to you at all, considering who you brought back into town."

If Justine hadn't felt physically ill before, she did now. She looked at her brother, but he avoided eye contact.

"Mitzy, please," Devlin said through his teeth. "I need a minute with Justine—"

"He's changed, you know," Mitzy said, purposely blind to Devlin's growing panic. "He looks every bit as fascinating and dangerous as ever, but man, oh, man, does he get more gorgeous over time."

"Mitzy," Devlin said warningly.

Justine gripped her glass with both hands, wondering whom everyone was discussing. But her brother's strange behavior and pallor worried her, and he, as always, came first. "I'm sorry," she said as politely as she could to Mitzy. "We were just leaving—"

"Oh, but you can't, not yet," Mitzy declared, her eyes lighting up. "Not before I introduce you to my guest of honor. Ah, and here he is now." She smiled brilliantly at a person just behind Justine.

Next to her, Devlin groaned and closed his eyes.

Someone came up directly behind Justine, and for some inexplicable reason, her every nerve ending tingled with a strange sense of awareness. She hadn't had that happen since—

"Justine, I'm sure you remember Mitchell Conner. Mitch," she purred, lifting a hand toward Justine, "here's the pride of the *Heather Bay Daily News*, our own Justine Miller."

No. Please, God, no. Knees knocking, Justine turned to face the one and only man who'd ever broken her heart, the only man to have shattered her dreams.

Mitch's deep green eyes softened as she looked at him. His mouth curved into the familiar crooked smile that had never failed to render her deaf, blind, and dumb. "Hello, Jussie."

At the husky, unbearably endearing sound of his voice, memories slammed into her, leaving her shaky and unwilling to trust her own voice.

"Oh, good," Mitzy said, clapping her hands together. "You *do* recognize each other."

Recognize each other? If Justine weren't so shell-shocked, she would've laughed hysterically. Instead, the delicate crystal goblet she held slipped through her damp hands and shattered at their feet, splashing champagne over their shoes.

"Oops!" Mitzy laughed. "Looks like our Justine is clumsy as ever."

Justine swallowed hard and glanced down, struggling to remember to breathe.

"Justine," Devlin broke in, but she just shook her head sharply, needing a minute.

He looked the same, she thought, her heart pounding frantically in her ears. God, he looked the same. Tall. A thick mane of dark hair that he still wore on the wrong side of too long. Amazing green eyes that could charm the light right out of the moon and the tough, rugged body of a trained athlete.

But Mitch was much, much more than an athlete. Or at least, he had been. Yet that had been two long years ago. She had no idea what he was now.

No idea at all.

With the poise born of pure desperation and far too much pride, Justine lifted her chin, making a sound of half amusement, half disdain. "Of course I remember him, Mitzy. How could I forget my own husband?"

TWO

Ignoring their rapt audience, Mitch shifted closer to the woman who had haunted his dreams for two long years. She was far more beautiful than he remembered. The dress that hugged her body nearly took his breath away. Still petite and trim, she'd matured in all the right places, gaining soft, lush curves that made his mouth go dry.

But she hid his favorite part of her, the part that was the window to her heart, the mirror of his own soul—her incredible sky-blue eyes. Palms sweaty, heart roaring, blood pumping, he reached out, wanting to haul her close and never let go.

That they were surrounded by dozens of people didn't stop him from touching her, nor did the fact that Justine was staring intently down at the splintered glass at her feet as if it held the greatest interest to her. *As if her husband hadn't disappeared on their wedding night and just now reappeared.* No, what completely galvanized him was the single tear that trickled down one satiny cheek.

Justine Miller never cried.

"Jussie," he whispered, dropping his hand helplessly.

"We heard the gossip," Mitzy said gleefully, rubbing her hands together. "Is it true, Mitch? Are you the new owner of the *Daily News*?"

Justine gasped. With a whirl of her glorious fire-gold hair, she jerked her head up and looked at him at last. "*What?* What did she just say?"

Every four-letter word he could think of crossed Mitch's brain, and then some. This confrontation was going to be difficult enough without interference, and if he could have gotten away with it, he would have cheerfully strangled Mitzy. "Justine," he said quietly, keeping his gaze steady on her furious one. "I'd like to speak to you. Privately."

The wide range of emotions that crossed her face then fascinated him. Confusion, horror, rage . . . bitter hurt—each one stabbed at him.

"I'm sure Justine will be thrilled to have your support at the paper. She's still trying to prove herself. It's probably because people love to compare her with her father, even after all this time." Mitzy batted her long, black lashes. "Oh, my, the psychiatrists would have a field day with that one, wouldn't they?"

Without a word in response, Justine turned to her brother. "Devlin?" A choked laugh escaped her. "What the hell is going on?"

"Ah . . ." Devlin bit his lip. "I wanted to tell you—"

"Tell me what?" She leaned close to be heard over the joyful and very off-key rendition of "Jingle Bells" directly behind them. "That the man who deserted me is alive? That you apparently knew where he was? Or that you sold the one thing I had left in this world to care about—to *him*?"

All right, he couldn't stand it. Mitch had to get her alone, had to explain and make her understand. He had to, because he couldn't handle the anguish in her voice. Leaning toward Mitzy to be heard, he said in a firm voice, "Obviously, we need a few minutes."

She nodded, and didn't budge.

"*Alone*," he added, waiting until she reluctantly retreated to a waiting group of women who were quite clearly hoping for the "scoop."

Relieved, Mitch took a deep breath and looked at Justine. For a minute he caught her unguarded expression as she looked at him in return, and time stood still. He was transported back to his wedding day. To the incredible vision Justine had been in white silk and flowers. To the hope and warmth and joy he'd felt as he watched her walk slowly toward him, love shining in her eyes. Love for him. She'd been the first and last ever to give him that emotion, and the hope that her love had survived these two years was all that had kept him alive.

Then Justine blinked, and the hurt and mistrust came back in a flash.

"Is it true?" she said to Devlin, her petite hands fisted at her sides. "You sold the *Daily News* to *him*?" She jerked her shoulder toward the "him" in question.

"Well . . ."

"Devlin!"

"It's true," Mitch said. Gently, he took her bare elbow and turned her back to face him. Simply touching her made his hand shake. Her skin felt incredibly soft. She wore the same scent, that irresistible blend of innocence and sensuality that drove him wild. "The paper is mine. But I only bought it because—"

"*I asked my brother.*" Each word was grated out through clenched teeth. The glass at their feet crunched as she yanked her arm free and backed up a step. Her chest heaved with each breath, and the already plunging neckline of her dress sank even lower, making him wonder just how secure she was in that gown.

"Ask *me*, Jussie," he said, aching at the hurt on her face. "I'm standing right here. You can't ignore me forever."

"Why not?" she shot back. "You've ignored me for two years."

Sorrow drove him, just as desperation and fear had for each of those years she spoke of. "Not by choice, believe me!"

Lifting her chin, she leveled an ice-hard gaze on him. "I don't want to hear this. All I want to know is how you conned Devlin into giving you the paper. It's ours!"

Mitch had to get them outside, and quickly. The caroling had stopped. So had most of the nearby conversation. A curious crowd was starting to gather. A glance at Devlin told Mitch he could expect backup, if necessary. "Jussie, let's go. We'll talk at home."

She laughed bitterly, but she didn't miss the attention they were beginning to draw. "We have no home," she whispered. "Not after next week, anyway."

"Fine," he said softly, hating himself for not being around when she'd so obviously needed him. But he was here now, and he was here to stay. "You pick the place and we'll go. But we need to talk."

Jaw rigid, shoulders impossibly square, and eyes unnaturally bright, Justine shrugged free of the arm he offered and walked through the crowd. Mitch followed, unable to bite back his proud smile as he watched her face down a room full of people dying of curiosity. *This* was his Jussie, the woman who'd faced enough losses in her short lifetime to bring anyone else to their knees.

She remained silent as she collected her wrap. Halfway through the parking lot, she stopped short. "Where's Devlin? I need to kill him."

"He knows we need to talk alone."

"But—"

"*Alone.*" The moonlight slashed through the black winter night, lighting her face clearly. The myriad emotions he found there broke his heart.

"I'm not going anywhere with you," she said stubbornly. She crossed her arms and gave him a dark scowl. "I don't know how I'll manage this, but I'm buying back the *Daily News* from you. So just go back to wherever you've been and . . ." Her voice hitched, but when he reached for her, she backed up a step. "And leave me alone," she finished on a choked whisper, not meeting his gaze.

"I can't do that," he said quietly, determined to get through to her. "My God, Jussie, I've dreamed of this. The past two years, my entire life has been centered around this moment, and what you'd do when I saw you again for the first time." He waited a beat. "I have to admit, I never pictured getting a shoe shine in champagne."

She didn't smile, didn't budge, and he sighed silently. He'd expected her to be difficult, but not impossible. He should have known. Jussie never gave in easy.

"Much as I fantasized," he went on, "I never pictured you as beautiful as you look right now."

She let out a disparaging sound that tore at him. Her shoulders hunched defensively, as if warding off a blow, making him yearn to comfort her.

"I know you're hurt," he said. "And bitter. But when the FBI explained this to you, they—"

"What?" She scowled and blinked. "What FBI?"

He stared at her. "After I left, the FBI came and told you what happened. They explained why there could be no contact."

Slowly, her eyes never leaving his, she shook her head. "No. No one came."

Shock hit him first. He'd never expected this. They'd never explained his absence to her. They'd let her think . . . My God, he thought as fury filled him. They'd let her think he'd just left without reason. He wanted to yell, swear, hit something. All of which would get him nowhere with the woman looking at him as if he were pond scum.

It took every ounce of control he had to stay calm. "I'm sorry," he said with great inadequacy, feeling completely helpless. She hadn't known anything except he'd disappeared. He'd been miserable the past two years without her, but at least *he'd* known what had happened.

She'd known nothing.

"This . . . is just too much for me to take in all at once." Justine swallowed hard and hugged herself.

He rushed to soothe her before she could bolt. "Your speed, Jussie. We can go at your speed."

"I have so many questions."

"I know. I can answer them."

Her smile was bittersweet as she shook her head. "I don't think so, Mitch. It's been too long."

"No. I don't believe that." Didn't want to believe that. For as long as he could remember, she'd been the only one. The only one to want him unconditionally, befriend him, *love* him. It couldn't be too late. His hands went damp. "Jussie, I won't believe it."

"You don't have a choice." She took a step backward. "You left me. It's my decision now, Mitch."

With each step she took, she moved farther away from him. How could he let her walk away? Yet to offer her the pathetic excuse that his superiors had let him down wouldn't appease her. Not at all. "Are you saying you can look at me and feel nothing?" he urged.

She went still.

"That your hurt and pride are more important than getting those answers you deserve?" he pressed, needing to know the answer. "That I could walk away again and you'd be fine?"

She lifted her chin. "That's what I'm saying. I'm fine. And seeing you again didn't hurt near as much as I thought it would."

"You know, that's the first lie I think I've ever heard you tell," he said with great disappointment.

She looked at him for a long moment. "I really hate that you can still do that."

"Do what? Understand you so well? I always did, Jussie." Could she not see his heart? He was wearing it right on his sleeve. "Just as you always understood me. It's what made us such an incredible team."

Without a word, she turned and starting walking.

Panic welled in him with each step she took. He had to stop her, but short of force, he had only words. "You never divorced me."

She froze, but didn't turn to face him. "Don't tempt me."

"You claim to feel nothing," he said gruffly. "So why didn't you?"

Silence.

"Jussie?"

"I never claimed to feel nothing." She spoke so reluctantly, so low and husky, Mitch could hardly hear her, but hope soared within him. He wished she'd look at him.

"You're still wearing your wedding band," she said to the night sky.

He wiggled the gold band on his finger. "I've never taken it off." But *she* had, he'd noticed. Her fingers were ring-free.

"You never divorced *me* either," she said, head still bowed. Her hair had fallen forward, exposing the sweet, vulnerable nape of her neck, making him want to put his lips to that exact spot.

"Why didn't you?" came her soft voice.

He'd spent the last two years in hell. Being married to Justine had been just about all he'd had. "I couldn't. But I'm glad, Jussie, so very glad we're still married."

Now she did turn to face him. "The marriage wasn't . . . consummated."

"Maybe not after the ceremony, but certainly enough times before." He didn't need more light to see her blush. He felt the heat, too, as an image of that last summer came to him. Jussie, sprawled on his bed wearing nothing but a shy, teasing smile. Her hair blanketing his pillow, her lovely body writhing beneath his.

Her voice, soft and tortured, broke the spell. "You

can't just waltz back in here after all this time and expect me to want to reminisce."

"Are you happy?"

The question clearly caught her off guard. Her arms fell to her sides. She studied her shoes. "Go away," she whispered finally. "Please, just go away."

Instead, he walked to her. "Aren't you curious about where I was?" He was desperate to tell her everything, terrified she wouldn't let him. "Even a tiny bit?"

The Justine he'd known had been incapable of lying, and it thrilled him to know it was still true.

"Yes," she said so softly, he had to lean closer. "I am. But—"

"No buts." Gently, he took her hand. "Come on, Jussie. We've known each other forever."

"I didn't meet you until I was fifteen."

She'd been a high-school freshman, the bookworm. Alone against the world, with only her younger brother on her side. Mitch had been without any family at all, but never alone. He'd been a senior stuck on girls, basketball, and more girls, and the king of the class. To the parents of Heather Bay, he'd been the proverbial bad boy, completely without supervision. But though he'd been a loner at heart, the kids in school, both boys and girls, hadn't been able to get enough of him. Despite his tendency to stick to himself, he was intensely popular.

"You helped me pass English lit," he remembered.

She snorted. "Like you couldn't have *taught* that class."

He'd taken one look at the young, sweet girl sitting in the quad, the one always neat as a pin, the one who never cheated, never said a bad word about anyone, who never gave any boy in the school a second glance, and he'd lost his heart.

He hadn't been able to help feigning ignorance about Shakespeare to get the compassionate Justine to feel sympathy for him, to spend time with him. She'd tutored him that semester, all sweet shyness, long beautiful hair, and glorious blue eyes, so big he could have jumped in and happily drowned. In between the vast responsibilities of caring for her brother, working at the paper, and keeping up with her extra-credit classes, she'd given him all the time she could spare.

Her generosity warmed him, opened him up to a storm of emotions he hadn't expected. It wasn't until she'd discovered his history of straight A's that Mitch had gotten his first taste of her formidable temper. He'd fallen the rest of the way in love with her on the spot.

Now, over a decade later, he looked into her eyes, finding more than a little of that temper stirring.

"You promised you'd never lie to me again," she said.

"I haven't."

"Hmmph."

"I haven't," he repeated firmly.

Two simple words, and even Justine, with her heart purposely hardened, *had* to hear the honesty in them. He hoped.

"No. I won't give in to this."

"Jussie," he said, frustrated. "You're going to have to listen—"

"No." Stubborn to the end, she crossed her arms. No matter what her sharp journalistic instincts had to be screaming, she wouldn't listen. But the heart-pounding, soul-baring emotion in her gaze killed him.

She crossed her arms tighter around herself. "Please, Mitch."

She'd asked the wrong man for mercy. "Whatever happened to the girl who'd never turn down the chance for a hot scoop?" he wondered, lifting a brow.

The dare worked, but not quite in the way he'd hoped. Her eyes went icy again. "Oh, she lives," she assured him. "But she's ruthless now. And quite possibly unemployed. Are you sure you're ready?"

Hard, hot, and dying. She had no idea just how ready he was. "Oh, I'm ready, Jussie." Never in his wildest hopes had he allowed himself to think it would be so easy, though the fury barely banked in her gaze had tension rippling through his body.

"Still a navy SEAL?"

He blinked. "What?"

"I said, are you still a—"

"What does this have to do with our getting back together?"

She stared at him, then let out a short laugh. "Back together?"

"Yes," he said curtly. "You just said—"

"I said I'm ready to get my hot scoop." Her hands bracketed her hips. "And that's *all* I'm ready for. Are you going to give it to me or not?"

"I can't."

Her eyes narrowed. "Why not?"

"It has to be off the record."

"Why?" she demanded. "Still hate publicity? It's a little late for that, after the entrance you made."

He couldn't handle the hostility in her eyes. "I want to talk to *you*, not the entire population of Heather Bay."

"Then why did you show up like that? You knew everyone would be there, you knew we'd draw a crowd."

"I had to see you right away."

He didn't add that he'd come to her as soon as he could. The threat to him was gone, and Hopkins had released him from both the Federal Witness Protection Program and his obligation as a special agent for the FBI. Reluctantly, but he'd done it. "I knew if I showed up at your house or at work, you'd refuse to listen."

"You have no idea how I'd react to anything. Not anymore."

There was a hitch in her breathing he was afraid to analyze. "Jussie—"

"No. We're over." Her voice wavered and he leaped on that.

"I can explain—"

"I know," she said sadly. "And the worst thing is, I'd probably believe you, fool that I am. I used to dream about it, you know. Pretend that you'd *had* to go away."

"But—"

"Don't you *dare* tell me you were a protected witness or something," she warned, coming so close to the truth, he winced. "I've seen too many movies. I won't believe you."

"You're making a mistake," he said very softly, knowing her well enough to keep his own temper in check.

"We're over. Completely over. *The end.*"

"No." Yet he knew, even as she whirled and raced away, her heels clicking loudly in the asphalt lot, that he'd lost this round.

He drew a deep breath, felt the band of tension

around his chest. "This isn't the end, Jussie," he whispered. "Not by a long shot. It's just the beginning."

He waited until he saw her pull safely out of the lot before heading to his car to grab his cell phone. It wasn't easy to grip it without crushing it, to hit the numbers calmly and efficiently, when he wanted to rant and rave.

Jussie hadn't been told about what happened to him, and he wanted to know why.

THREE

The alarm went off the next morning and Justine groaned. She hadn't slept a wink. Nightmares reminding her of painful losses had kept her up. So had memories of the marriage she'd once wanted with all her heart, and the unwanted, terrifying excitement at seeing Mitchell Conner again.

She'd watched every half hour tick by on the clock all night, and she figured she'd gotten no more than an hour or so of solid sleep.

It wasn't nearly enough, but it would have to do. Much as a small part of her wanted to hide beneath her covers, the fighter in her needed to face what was happening.

Despite her exhaustion, she forced herself to run the two miles that preceded every morning's shower. Then she dressed, plotting out who she'd tackle first, Devlin or *him*.

She opted for Devlin, since she wasn't so anxious to

experience that gut-wrenching sensation of seeing her soon-to-be ex-husband again.

Her low-heeled sensible shoes clicked loudly as she ran up the brick steps of the Daily News Building. It'd been in her family for four decades, and a Miller had been at the helm during that entire time, except for the brief lapse between her father's death and her own reign. She'd been too young to edit the paper at the tender age of twelve, but it had been only a matter of time and education before she had.

The *Daily News* was her joy, her work, her life. Always had been. Just yesterday she might have said raising Devlin equaled it, but now confusion and hurt had her reserving judgment.

Why had he sold the one thing she cared about above all else—and to the man who'd once destroyed her heart and soul? How could he have?

But Justine hadn't gotten through her life by dwelling on things, whether she had reason to or not. With a forced calm—she was teaching herself to be calm, though last night her discipline had taken a bad beating—she smoothed down her skirt and entered the building.

As always, the hallways buzzed with activity, the phones jangled, and people practically ran, not walked, in all directions.

Chaos, wonderful, out-of-control chaos.

And the center of her universe. Always, she'd loved it here, felt at home. And always, just the smell of ink and excitement had been enough to soothe her.

Until now.

She decided that Devlin most likely had hidden out

here last night, since he certainly hadn't come home, the *chicken*. Just the thought riled her again.

"Justine?"

Reluctantly, she turned to face Jack Nottingham, her chief financial officer and loyal friend. "Jack."

He smiled. "Morning."

With the set of mechanical pencils in the breast pocket of his white oxford shirt and the files and calculator in his hands, Jack looked the picture of a polished, well-respected accountant. He was also the sweetest, most caring man Justine had ever met.

She knew from the way he often looked at her that it would take little more than an encouraging smile to make their relationship far more than platonic, but she'd never been able to take that step.

Her heart was dead.

Though at the moment it had been cruelly brought back to life—blazing, painful life. "I'm sorry," Justine said now in the most civil voice she could manage when bad temper and no sleep rattled every bone in her body. "Our weekly budget meeting's going to have to be postponed." She struggled to remember what else they'd planned for today. "So does fiscal planning."

Jack smiled sympathetically and moved closer, his worried gaze aimed directly at her. "Don't worry about it. You're looking for Devlin."

Good Lord. Did the entire town know what had happened last night? Of course they did, she thought bitterly. Thanks to her no-good, *very*-soon-to-be ex-husband, she'd become the laughingstock of the town.

"Is he here?" She tried to sound casual, and probably succeeded. After all, she was the master of taking control, of hiding her feelings. It'd been her survival tactic for several years.

"Not yet."

Not yet. Where was he then? Devlin, like his sister, didn't deal well with confrontation. The trouble she was in at this moment attested to that.

"Justine." Jack touched her shoulder until she looked at him. His eyes were dark chocolate, warm and friendly, contrasting sharply with his smooth blond hair, elegant clothes, and the sophisticated image he projected. "You're not going to get any peace in your office."

"I'm not expecting any."

"Come to mine," he suggested, with the kind, undemanding smile she'd come to appreciate. "I've got raspberry tea."

Her favorite. "Jack."

Now he grinned coaxingly. "And doughnuts."

Tea. Talk. Budgets. Fiscal planning. Doughnuts. All delivered with a sympathy she simply couldn't handle. A sudden lump in her throat threatened to choke her, yet she ruthlessly stomped on her own self-pity and lifted her chin. "Thanks. But I've got to . . ." She couldn't very well announce the plans she had made for the slow, painful death of both her brother and the man she couldn't even think about without wanting to cry. "I need to work on that reappointment piece I'm doing."

He nodded easily, but gently squeezed her shoulder, his gaze probing deep. "You okay?"

"Of course."

Jack glanced around. Apparently satisfied that no one listened, he said softly, "It's got to be a shock, Justine."

She wondered which shock he referred to. That she'd let her brother bankrupt them, or that the man she thought she'd finally gotten over had dared to reenter her life and turn it upside down. "I'm really fine. Quite fine."

"But—"

"And I need to be alone," she said quickly, stepping back so that his hand fell from her shoulder. Any more sympathy and she'd fall apart. She was simply too close to the edge. One more kind word might send her over, and she'd die before she allowed herself to lose it here in front of a member of her staff, friend or not.

Jack's expression reflected his disappointment, but she knew he wouldn't push. It was what she liked most about him, it was what made him "safe."

As he had been for some time. The pang of guilt wasn't expected. Yes, they'd been fast friends. And yes, they'd spent every Monday morning together for the past two years, chatting about business plans and weekend activities. But it didn't mean she had to tell all.

She couldn't, not even to herself. "I appreciate your concern, but I'm just fine."

"All right. You know I'm here if you need anything," he said, waiting a beat. When she didn't respond, he let out a small sorrow-filled smile and left her alone.

Justine managed to avoid any awkward questions by hurrying to her office, but she hadn't missed the quick surge of curiosity in the clerk's gaze as she'd passed her in the hallway. Or the way everyone in marketing had stopped talking when she'd passed their group. Sighing with resignation, she leaned against her closed door for a long moment before taking a deep breath and walking to her desk.

Messages were waiting, nothing unusual. She wasn't

surprised to see that five of them were urgent and from Mitzy. *Call me*, they all said. *It's important*.

"Yeah, right," she muttered, and filed the messages in the trash can beneath her desk.

The morning edition had been left on her desk. Instead of being neatly folded, it lay open. Covering the front picture was a sticky note from Anne, her loyal and hardworking secretary.

Sorry, Justine. But you did hold space for whatever picture Mitzy brought back from the party. Looks like she picked a doozy.

Dread had Justine pulling off the note slowly, but she still hadn't properly prepared herself. Dropping bonelessly into her chair, which luckily was directly behind her, she stared at the social section.

A large picture from the party stared back at her; of herself in that gold evening dress she'd never wear again, no matter how much the darn thing had cost. She stood in a circle with her brother, Mitzy, and *him*. The horror and disbelief on Justine's face as she stared at Mitchell Conner was rendered only more dramatic by the fact that her glass of champagne seemed to be floating between her hand and the hard floor, halfway to shattering at their feet.

The caption read, HEATHER BAY'S BAD BOY IS BACK, READY FOR HONEYMOON.

Justine groaned and snatched up the paper, pulling it closer to her face for a better look. Devlin's face registered alarm and . . . yes, that was fear. Damn him. Mitzy looked wickedly pleased, damn her too. But Mitch, he had eyes for no one but herself as his photographic image stared at her with a mixture of heat, need, and an unbearable hunger she'd thought never to see again. And the paper had caught every bit of it, magnifying each emotion, so that every Heather Bay citizen could study it over their morning coffee.

She crushed the paper between her hands as her temper surged. With rage and hurt guiding her, she grabbed a match from her desk drawer and struck it. Then, holding the paper over her trash can, she smiled with satisfaction as she slowly brought the match to the paper.

"Good morning."

She nearly leaped out of her skin as the man invading her thoughts strode into the room. By his smile, she'd guess he didn't have a care in the world. He certainly looked far better than a wife deserter should look.

"God, it's good to see you," Mitch said warmly. His smile made her legs wobble.

It would have been far easier to hate him if he wasn't so devastatingly *present*. So vivid. So absolutely male. His dark hair curled over his collar. His eyes, the color of drenched moss, smiled as if he were recalling a private joke. Even the hollows and planes of his face drew attention. His mouth was firm now, but she knew that could change with no warning, nudging emotions from her with one crooked grin.

He arched a dark eyebrow at the sight she must have made, leaning over the trash, holding a wadded paper in one hand, a lit match in the other. "Hmm. Saw the paper already, did you?" He tsked low in his throat as he leaned against her desk, crossing his arms over his wide chest. "Not very loyal around here, are they?"

It was hard to think, she discovered, with her heart blocking her windpipe.

The man driving her to insanity didn't seem to have

that problem. In fact, he just continued to smile. "So, how's my wife this morning?"

The unattended match burned down to her fingers. "Ouch!" She swore and dropped the match, bringing her singed fingers to her mouth. The paper fell harmlessly to the floor.

Mitch was there instantly, taking her wrist in his strong hand, inspecting her now-wet fingers. He bent over her, looking at her skin intently. His soft breath brushing her skin pushed her irritation into full-blown anger.

"They're fine," she said with exasperation, trying unsuccessfully to yank them back. He even smelled good, she thought resentfully. Soapy, earthy, and one hundred percent masculine. *The jerk.* "Let me go."

More to continue touching her than anything else, Mitch held on and decided to bear the fury that flashed in her eyes. He'd worked through that temper plenty of times in the past, and he could only hope he still had the knack for soothing it. "You look good, Jussie." With his other hand, he cupped her cheek. "Real good."

She blinked, clearly flustered. Then she slapped his hand away. "Don't."

"Don't what?" he asked pleasantly. "Don't look at you? Or don't say nice things?"

"Either," she said, scowling when he laughed. "And while you're at it, go away. I've got work to do." She paled a bit. "If I still have a job."

His good humor slipped. "You think I can know how much the paper means to you, and take away your job?"

"I don't know what to think," she said quietly.

Mitch looked at her carefully, seeing the faint purple circles beneath her eyes, the wariness etched in her eyes.

Exhaustion, he thought with remorse. His fault. And Hopkins's as well. His ex-superior had tried to placate Mitch last night, had tried to explain how the little detail of informing Jussie had gotten missed, but he wasn't having any of it.

It left him in a hell of a position with this temperamental, angry woman he wanted so desperately back in his life. "We need to talk."

She straightened her already impossibly straight shoulders. "I told you last night, I don't think so."

It was hard, he found, so very hard to face the hostility in her gaze, when all he wanted to see was love and affection. Oh, he'd been in difficult situations before, especially during the past two years, but nothing had been as tough as this. *Nothing* was as soul wrenching as standing here looking into the eyes of the woman he loved more than his own life, and seeing only fury, confusion, and hurt—all of which *he'd* caused. Feeling low as a snake, he ran his thumb lightly over the base of her wrist.

Her head was bowed, so he couldn't see her face, and she barely came up to his shoulders. So petite, so vulnerable . . . and her skin so soft and creamy he had to force himself not to bend and taste it. "You'll have to listen to me sometime, Jussie. We have too much of a past for you not to."

Beneath his softly caressing finger, the pulse at her wrist was frantic, giving him a surge of relief—he could still affect her.

"I don't *have* to do anything," she assured him, trying again to pull back. "Especially listen to any weak excuse for bailing out on our marriage. Stop touching me, damn you."

The pleasure he'd felt at her body's response to him dissipated, and for a minute he could only stare at her. "Is that what you think?" he asked roughly, hurt to the core. "That I didn't want you?"

"What does it matter?"

This time when she pulled her hand back, he let go. "Oh, it matters," he said grimly, unprepared. She'd actually believed that he'd left her on purpose. Of course she would. After all, he'd disappeared without a trace. But he'd hoped she would realize what had happened had been out of his control. "Jussie, you can't believe I *wanted* to stay away."

The look in her eyes told him that's exactly what she believed.

He thought of the past two sleepless years, when not more than a few minutes had gone by at any given time when he hadn't thought of her, dreamed of her, yearned for her. "I didn't *want* to stay away. I did only because—"

"Stop!" she cried, lifting her hands to her ears. "I don't want to hear it."

She'd always stood by him, when he'd entered the navy, when he'd become a SEAL, when he'd dreamed of happily ever after, with her. Always, she'd been part of his plans. Now she wanted him to leave her alone? "I can't stop," he said carefully. "And I can't believe you won't listen to me. The Jussie I remember listened to everyone. You have the sweetest, most giving heart of anyone I know."

"I have no heart," she said firmly, startling him. She stepped away, putting distance between them. Crossing her arms over her middle, she stared miserably out the window.

He wanted to see her smile, all the way to her glorious blue eyes. Smile for him, at him, with him, but that wasn't going to happen, not today. Sighing, he stepped up behind her, heart aching at the way she stiffened.

"All right," she said wearily. "I can see you're not going to leave me alone until I listen. Let's have it. Give me the scoop." She spoke quite calmly, in complete opposition to the tension radiating from her.

"The scoop?"

"Yes." She nodded coolly. "The paper could use a good one. All I've had lately is some dirt on the mayor that no one seems to want to read about anyway."

"No," he said so harshly her head whipped up in surprise. "I told you last night, this isn't a story for public consumption, Jussie. Only for you. I can't tell you until you promise me."

"I won't make that promise. You don't deserve it."

She put just enough spite in her words to spark his own temper. Two years of doing nothing but alternately sweating in fear and longing for her, and she could say *that*? "You have no idea what I deserve."

No, she didn't. But if she listened to what he wanted to tell her so badly, she'd lose control. She'd get hurt. Again. She refused to allow it to happen, knowing she would never survive it this time. Never. "This paper was mine," she whispered. "*Mine*. My entire life, it's all I ever wanted."

He knew that, which only made it all the harder to stand there and watch her suffer. "It's still yours. I'm not taking it from you."

"You own it."

"Only because you can't!" He lowered his voice. "I

don't care whose name is on the contract, Jussie. It's yours."

She looked unconvinced. And mad as hell.

"You can buy it back when you're able, if it makes you feel better; I don't care," he said. "Then we'll—"

"No. No *we*," she blurted, looking panicked at the thought. "I can't handle a *we*."

His jaw tightened. Impatient and stressed, he rolled his shoulders.

She made a sound and looked unnerved.

"What?"

"Nothing." But her own shoulders sagged. "Everything. You always did that," she accused, pointing at him. "Shrugged like that."

"Did I?" he asked, both surprised and pleased she remembered him so well.

She looked miserable. "Sometimes you look so . . . familiar."

Hope had his heart pumping. Until she spoke.

"I don't want to work for you." She fisted her hands at her sides. "I don't want to see you."

"I know." He didn't dare touch her, though he wanted to. "Look, you needed help, and I was in a position to give it. Isn't it better, easier, to take it from me than from a perfect stranger who might have taken your job as well?"

"No."

"God, you're stubborn. You still have that amazing self-control. It's admirable. Really," he added when she lifted a doubtful eyebrow. "As long as I've known you, it's what's driven you. But it's okay to give it up, you know. Just a little. It's okay to lean on someone once in a while."

From her perch at the window, she said nothing. Her hair, the color of a fiery sunset, had been pulled back into a twist. Like her office, she was meticulous and tidy. Efficient, but not distant. Never distant, even now. No one would take a look at those flashing eyes and expression-filled face and consider her without feelings, much as she might wish it so. She wore a neat blouse, tucked into an equally neat skirt that hid most of her perfect legs. There was little makeup on her classically beautiful face, made cute by her small, turned-up nose. Just a touch of color on those lips he wanted to feel beneath his, and a hint of that scent she wore. The one that made him want to swallow her whole.

"This is a bad idea," she said. "Working together."

"Of course it's not." He had to convince her to stay, or she'd never stand still long enough for him to make up the past to her. "You're the editor in chief here. No one else will do."

"I love my job," she admitted, her voice husky with emotion. "More than you could possibly know. But—"

"Why do you say that?" he wondered, interrupting her. "I've known you for years, and that entire time all you've ever wanted is to be right where you are at this moment. Why would you think I couldn't understand your love for this job?"

"Because you don't know me anymore. I'm not the same woman I was."

He doubted that. She'd always been loyal, steadfast, strong as a rock, and the most compassionate woman in the world. From what he could tell, nothing had changed. "The job is yours," he said softly. "I only bought the paper to help you."

Wrong thing to say, he realized as she sprang to action, stalking away from him to pace the area in front of her desk.

"To help me," she repeated. "You bought the paper to help me." Her long legs churned up the carpet as she moved. "Well, I don't want your pity, so go away and don't come back this time. Forget the scoop, it's not worth it."

He couldn't stop himself from grabbing her arm, and he caught her as she tried to whirl away. He towered over her, the top of her head barely reaching his chin. Even so, he knew by the flash of fury in her face that it was pure anger, not fear, that had her fighting him like a mad dog.

"Look." He swore as she kicked his shin, hard. "I have things to say to you—ouch!" She'd kicked him again, leaving him no choice but to haul her up against him and wrap his arms tightly around her. "I didn't leave you on purpose. I *had* to go. I was in the Witness Protection Program!"

"Yeah, right. If you didn't want to get married, you should have just said so," she said, struggling. "You didn't have to disappear after the ceremony, making a fool out of me."

"It's true, dammit." He lifted her clean off her feet, banding her close, rendering her immobile. Her body against his created a friction that startled him.

He found himself staring at her stupidly. He couldn't help it; having her soft, sweet body snug against his for the first time in too long had all the blood draining from his head down to a more prominent area.

At his unmistakable reaction, her eyes darkened, her full lips trembled open. Her breath caught, and for a long, telling moment neither of them moved.

"Jussie," he whispered hoarsely, bending his head to hers. He had to kiss her or die. Light as a feather, he stroked her mouth with his, closing his eyes as a wave of longing and desire hit him like a ton of bricks. She forgot to fight him, and he pressed his advantage, deepening the kiss. She slid closer, her lips parting, her soul opening to him as she surrendered. Humbled to his depths, and overwhelmed by the glimpse of what he'd wanted for so long, Mitch drew her closer with shaking hands. She moaned, and the sound held both despair and wonder. Immediately, he gentled his hold, trailing his mouth over her jaw.

"It's still the same," he whispered, marveling at the feel of her skin. "It's still so hot between us."

"No." Without warning, she went ballistic again, fighting him violently. "No, it's not!"

"Stop it," he said, gasping when she jerked one of her knees up and nailed him in the inner thigh. He'd been a SEAL. He knew how to fight, how to kill. It had become instinctive, or so he thought. But all defensive training flew out the window in the face of Jussie's temper, and he scrambled to keep her against him. "Jussie—"

He dropped her on an oath when the next knee hit bull's-eye in his groin. As stars filled his head he heard her office door fling open. "Wait!" he gasped, blinking frantically past the haze of pain. "Please, wait."

That she hesitated cheered him a little, but only a very little. Hurt shone in her eyes. So did betrayal and a self-disgust he couldn't take.

"I didn't mean to let you—" She faltered. "I never meant to— I mean . . . You *kissed* me," she accused. "I'm . . . leaving now."

"Okay." He cleared his throat. "Don't worry about it."

Her pretty eyes narrowed and she touched her still-wet lips self-consciously. "Worry about what?"

He shrugged casually. Oh, she was a fighter, but so was he, especially when it came to something as important to him as Jussie was. "About what your staff will say when they see how furious you are, that they'll assume that anger is over me. No biggee; I'm sure it won't bother you in the least to have people whispering about us working together when you can't stand the sight of me."

She gaped at him.

"Not to mention your shirt's untucked and I've kissed your lipstick off, when you're usually neat as a pin. Nope. Don't give it a second thought. In fact, I doubt anyone will even notice your hair."

Her mouth opened. Then very carefully closed. Wordlessly, she shut the door again. She shoved her shirttail back into her waistband and smoothed her hair, but didn't replace the color on her lips. Pride warred with humility, and Mitch found it fascinating to watch.

"You may have a point," she eventually conceded through her teeth.

"Meaning?"

Those baby blues shot daggers in his direction. "Meaning this won't happen again."

He'd see about that. "And you'll work with me?" *Please, God.*

She dragged her lower lip across her teeth as she contemplated him, and Mitch's gaze hungrily followed the movement. He'd wondered whether their unbelievable sexual sizzle would still be there when he saw her again. His painfully aroused body gave him his answer.

"Yes, I'll work with you." The words were unrelentingly hard. "But only because I refuse to quit, and I can't afford to buy this paper back from you. *Yet*."

He smiled easily and felt like jumping for joy. It was a small victory, but he'd take it.

"I won't kiss you," she promised, eyeing him as if he was planning on jumping her. "Not ever again."

"Maybe you should reserve judgment until after I've told you again where I've been."

"You've told me enough. The rest doesn't matter to me one little bit."

"Don't lie," he said quietly.

"Fine," she exploded, raising her hands. Her chest heaved. "*Fine*. It matters. Too much. But I just can't—I don't want to—please. I need to think." She opened the door and disappeared.

Mitch let out the breath he'd been holding and plopped down on the couch along the wall of her office. Oh, yeah, he had a long way to go. He'd left the government for good with this homecoming, whether Hopkins and the agency wanted to believe that or not. But he still had to get Justine to believe him—believe why he'd left, and why he'd stayed away. His jubilation at being back faded some as he thought of the daunting task ahead of him. Of getting the woman who'd yet to refer to him by name to admit she'd loved him once.

That maybe she loved him still.

FOUR

She'd lost her mind. Yeah, that was it, Justine decided. It was the only excuse she had for the way she'd alternately sounded like a shrew, then thrown herself at *him*. She sighed and moved into the empty—thank God—copy room. Surrounded by soundproof glass, she sank into a chair and pretended to look busy for anyone who happened to pass by.

She'd lost her temper, big time, which had accomplished just one thing as far as she could see—she'd shown the infuriating man exactly how badly he'd hurt her.

Then she'd kissed him, *really* kissed him—or maybe he'd kissed her. It didn't matter, not when she'd seen fireworks explode behind her closed eyes and her world had tipped on its axis. Good Lord, he'd felt so good, so right, so absolutely hers. She'd actually gotten lost in time until he'd whispered her name in that deep, husky, unbearably sexy voice.

The snake.

He'd left her without a word, completely vanished off the face of the planet. *Witness Protection*. Right, and she was Tinker Bell. The truth was, he'd gotten cold feet and she'd been stupid enough to spend her entire savings on private investigators trying to find him. She'd actually been worried sick at first. Then fury had set in, and had never faded.

Dammit, she'd loved him with everything she'd had, with all her hopes and dreams, with all her youth. Well, she was no longer that young, and no longer had hopes and dreams—outside of the *Daily News*. But seeing him, touching him, hurt. She'd have to be more careful, learn how to rein in her feelings. If she didn't, the next time she'd be a sobbing, hysterical mess.

That couldn't happen. Justine Miller had pride, and yes, times were tough. But no one, especially what's-his-name, would watch her fall apart.

A sound on the glass had her looking up into Devlin's solemn gaze. He waved. "Hi," he mouthed, with a small smile that didn't quite reach his eyes.

Justine took a deep breath and nodded her head, indicating he could come in.

He did so, with obvious reluctance, and Justine couldn't keep back her wry smile. "I'm unarmed," she said when he shut the door behind him.

"Good thing." He eyed her carefully. "I thought I'd need a white flag."

"You do."

His long, lean frame braced against the copy machine. "I thought my death certificate would please you, but I couldn't bring myself to get one."

"It's not worth anything unless I get to do the killing," she said so blandly, he laughed.

"Now I know it's safe. If you were still mad, you wouldn't be joking."

"Who says I'm joking?"

He drew a deep breath. "Okay, let's hear it. Are you all right?"

It was a heartfelt question, worthy of much more than a sardonic response, but at the moment it was all she had. "I'm peachy, Dev. Really."

"I'm sorry," he said suddenly. He seemed to fold into himself as he covered his face with his hands. "God, Justine, I'm so sorry."

It killed her to see his sorrow, his pain. For so long, it'd been just the two of them. Having lost their mother at Devlin's birth, and their father five years later in a bank robbery gone bad, they'd had only each other to rely on. For the most part, that had involved Justine taking care of Devlin, and a true and deeply binding love abided. She put aside her anger and went to him.

He hugged her tightly, and she let him cling for a minute, knowing he needed it. "I worried about you last night." They'd grown up in a group foster home where they'd been treated well but distantly—exactly what was expected in a home with too many children.

Later, when Justine had turned eighteen, they'd moved back into the childhood home that had been kept in trust for them, where they'd lived ever since. In all that time Devlin had kept many late nights, but never once had he stayed out until morning. Never once had he tried to avoid her as he'd done since the party.

"It's all my fault," he said, eventually straightening and meeting her gaze. "Everything."

"That's likely," she agreed dryly, holding his hand. "Tell me."

"I made a bad investment."

"I know."

"Then I made another one trying to fix the first one," he said.

"I know that too."

"The house got taken back by the bank, Justine."

"Yes, and we're moving the day after Christmas," she said, losing some of her calm. "That's a done deal, and it's not why I almost had a heart attack last night."

"I just wanted to help."

"Helping would be to tell me what the hell is going on. Last night—" She broke off helplessly at the reminder. At what it had been like to stare into the eyes of a man she'd once loved beyond reason. "You betrayed me, Dev. Tell me why."

"I couldn't stand by and let you lose the paper, not when it means so much to you. So I tried to find a buyer who would let things stay as they were, with the same staff. But that proved to be far more difficult than I thought."

"What do you mean?"

"The only takers were much larger papers looking to swallow a smaller one up."

"You didn't tell me that," she murmured, thinking he'd been so positive. So sure he'd get them back out of their financial bind.

"You had so much to worry about, with losing the house and everything."

"That was never a problem," she countered. "We would never have been out on the streets. You wanted to move in with Ted and Matt anyway, and now you can. I'll find a small apartment."

"I should have told you," Devlin said quietly, watching her carefully.

"You still can."

"You're wondering at the part where Mitch comes in."

"It has crossed my mind."

Devlin studied his hands. "I couldn't stand that I'd lost everything you'd tried so hard to build up over the years."

"We've been over that. Get to the point, Dev."

"Okay." He drew a deep breath. "One of the people I considered taking a loan from was Mitzy's father."

"Mayor Thompson?" This was a surprise. The mayor had never made any secret of how he felt about Devlin, especially once Mitzy had become interested in him. *No one* was good enough for his beautiful, wildly sought-after socialite daughter, and certainly not a down-on-his-luck, sometime sportswriter.

Not to mention the articles the *Daily News* had been running, the ones suggesting that good-old-boy Mayor Thompson might have accepted illegal funds at his last election. Justine had written those articles herself, using information she'd gotten from anonymous tips passed along to a most surprising channel—Devlin.

He said, "I was over at their house one day when Mrs. Thompson came home, excited."

Mrs. Thompson ran the most successful real-estate business in town, mostly because she capitalized on her husband's political connections. "She must have made a big sale. Or gotten a big commission."

"Yeah," he said, watching her carefully. "She'd just sold the Conner place."

Mitch's childhood home. One of the biggest, most

beautiful houses in Heather Bay. Since Mitch's father had taken off years before, it had been empty, simply because the repossessing bank had never been able to sell it.

Until now.

For a moment Justine felt what Mitch would have felt—surprise, hurt, bafflement. Mitch had wanted that house for as long as she could remember, but he'd never been able to afford to buy it.

Devlin pulled his hand free of hers and took her shoulders, waiting until she met his bleak gaze. "Mitch bought that house for himself when he knew he was coming back here."

"So he found out you were in financial trouble and pounced," she said dully. "Son-of-a—"

"No." Devlin shook his head. "*I* went to *him*."

"How?"

He ducked his head. "Through Mrs. Thompson."

"She wouldn't have divulged a client's name."

Again, he avoided looking at her. "Mitzy helped me. But when I found Mitch, he'd been just about to find us." He braced himself. "He bought the paper as a favor to *me*."

When Justine had first brought Mitch into their lives, Devlin had been an angry young kid in desperate need of a positive male role model. Mitch had been a young man in equally desperate need of belonging. They'd become instant friends. Closer than friends. They'd bonded as brothers. For that, Justine had been grateful. She'd always been sure that it'd been mostly Mitch's doing that Devlin had turned out okay.

She had no idea why remembering that should cause a huge lump in her throat.

Devlin spoke softly, earnestly. "When he found out what had happened to us, he wanted to buy our house, too, but I knew I'd never be able to explain that to you."

"You—he—" She had to sit down. Backing away from her brother, she sank into a chair. Clearing her throat, she started again. "He owns me. You sold me to him."

"No! It's not like that at all," her brother said quickly. "Not at all. God, Jus, he's not the jerk you want him to be, I promise you. Just think about this, let him tell you what's happened to him—"

"I don't care."

"Liar." Devlin raised a red eyebrow. "I saw how you looked last night, Jus, when you saw him for the first time. You care. You care a lot."

She lifted her chin and tried to stare him down, even though he towered over her. "I do not."

He smiled sadly and tugged on a loose strand of her honey-red hair that matched his. "Don't you?"

She could only stare at him in dismay. Of course, she did. For a flash she'd been so ecstatic at the sight of the man she'd married, she couldn't breathe. She was hurt, not dead, and she'd have to be dead to not respond to Mitchell Conner.

But then reality had crashed down on her.

The trick was in not letting Mitch know how he affected her, because he was as sharp as they came. If she gave him anything, anything at all, he'd take everything.

The worst of it was, she'd let him touch her, then kissed him with enough hunger to show him exactly what she felt.

"You know, I realized something last night," Devlin

said slowly. "It was the first time I'd seen that look on your face—that really alive look—in two years."

She sighed, since there was no sense in denying the truth. "Doesn't mean I'm happy to see him, because I'm not."

"I understand that it hurts, but Jus . . . he's been through hell, too."

"He deserted me, Devlin." Dammit, her voice shook. "Just left me without a word."

"And no one knows better than I how you suffered," he said softly. "But he's suffered too. And he didn't desert you. You'd know that if you'd just listen to his story."

"I've listened."

"But you don't believe."

Surging to her feet, she paced the room. "Tell me." She rounded on him so fast, he blinked. "You want me to know so badly, let's hear it. All of it."

"I think Mitch should—"

"*You* tell me," she said emphatically, crossing her arms and glaring at him in the way she knew would make him squirm.

He did. "Okay, but only a little, because I promised. "You know that he'd been planning to leave the SEALs, but that they weren't thrilled with him going, that they were trying to keep him."

"Yes. Don't you dare tell me some story about them kidnapping him and keeping him these two years."

"What happened isn't all that different, believe me."

"Dev."

"All right. You know he wanted to be a private investigator. He wanted to be home more, for you and the kids you'd have."

It'd been their dream. Mitch would leave the high-risk world for a calmer one, while still doing what he did best. Justine would do what she'd always wanted to do—run the paper. "Yes." The fist around her heart tightened. "I knew."

"Well, he'd already been approached by the FBI to work for them."

"He'd refused."

Devlin's mouth tightened. "Apparently the government doesn't approve when a highly trained individual whose services they need wants to go civilian. They were pressuring him."

And he hadn't said a word. Justine could remember how it'd been back then for them. Young, idealistic, and full of expectations, they'd treasured every moment of those years they'd dated. They'd been high-school sweethearts, together since her fifteenth year. Wildly, madly in love.

Memories had her closing her eyes. Mitch waiting at the curb in his old beat-up convertible to take her and Devlin to school, ditching science class to make out behind the oak tree in the courtyard. Graduation, and their very private celebration on the coast beneath a velvety sky full of diamond stars. Making the most of every spare moment between Mitch's naval training and her college classes. She could remember dancing in his arms beneath a misty moon, him smiling that special smile of his—how strong he'd been, how gentle those big hands. They'd had friendship, love, then marriage, at least for a few short hours.

And then, it was over.

"He saw something he shouldn't," Devlin was saying. "He saw it with someone else, and that person was murdered for it. To keep alive, Mitch was forced to enter the Witness Protection Program."

Her reverie dissolved as her reporter's instincts sprang to life. "I thought he was making that part up."

Devlin shook his head, looking uneasy. "This needs to come from him, Jus. I'll go get—"

"No." She didn't know if she could face him yet. To combat the crazy emotions swirling inside her, she switched to business mode.

Which made Devlin all the more uneasy. "You've got that look, Justine. Like you're working. Knock it off. This isn't on the record."

She grabbed a piece of paper, yanked the pencil she always had behind her ear. "More."

"Justine."

She looked at him, firmly burying her hurt that Mitch hadn't bothered, or cared enough, to contact her in all this time—regardless of what had happened to him. The possibility that maybe he *couldn't* contact her refused to take hold in her protesting, hurting mind. "Why is he back now?"

"I need you to acknowledge that this is off the record. I promised."

"Well, *I* didn't. Besides, if he's back now, it must be safe."

"It is. Apparently the threat is gone." Devlin smiled at her. "He came for you as soon as he could. Cool, huh? It'll be like old times. When we were a family."

Justine stopped furiously scribbling notes for the story she could already envision. "No, it isn't 'cool.' " She gentled her voice. "Dev, it isn't going to be like before."

"But I just told you, it wasn't his fault."

She knew she hadn't been the only one aching after Mitch's abrupt departure. Devlin had been nearly as attached to Mitch as she. "There isn't going to be a happily-ever-after, Dev. I'm sorry."

"Why?"

Why. Because her heart couldn't take it. Because she refused to allow herself to believe that he couldn't have told her. Because one more mind-blowing kiss from Mitch and she'd throw herself at his mercy and beg for more, and she had far too much pride for that. "Because it's over. The end."

"He doesn't believe that."

She thought of how she was going to have to work for him, face him every day. There were going to have to be ground rules, many of them. "He will."

"No, 'he' won't."

Justine whirled at that terrifyingly tender voice.

Mitch shut the door as he came in. Leaning back against it, he slid his hands into his pockets and shot her that crooked smile.

She wished he hadn't. Her heart tugged, spasmed, and generally hurt like hell. All from a single look.

She turned her back to him and hugged herself. He was across the room, she told herself. All the way across. Yet she could feel the heat radiating off him. Or maybe it was bouncing between them like some kind of a sexual sound wave. The tension from it alone would surely kill her. "My brother and I were having a *private* conversation."

"About me," he said, sounding amused rather than threatened.

She risked a glance, and found him studying her intently, no sign of laughter on his face.

"It was personal," she said. "Go away."

With the ease of one trained for any situation, Mitch changed tactics. "This is my place now. I'm not going anywhere." He watched her shoulders stiffen and cursed himself for being an idiot.

"Good point," she murmured, obviously struggling to keep the bitterness out of her voice. "I'd better get to work."

Devlin moved ahead of her, and Mitch let him go, though they shared a long, wordless glance that told Mitch exactly how badly it had gone.

When Jussie tried to push past him, he stopped her.

Eyes like daggers, she glanced purposely down at the arm restraining her. Then she shot him a cool look, in perfect control as always.

"Let's talk," he said conversationally.

"I have to work, remember?" She shrugged him off, but not before he saw the hurt just beneath the anger.

Hurt and longing.

Without warning, he wanted to kiss her again.

She must have caught his intention, for her eyes widened and she stepped back from him, inadvertently ramming herself into the doorjamb. When he reached for her, she mumbled an oath and fled.

Justine hurried back to her office, flushed with embarrassment and mentally kicking herself with disbelief. She'd tried to prepare herself for the sight of him, and still she'd nearly let him kiss her again!

She sank into her chair, badly shaken. Mitch had been her entire life once, and that was the key word she needed to remember. *Once.*

When Mitch had left her, she'd been forced to go on. It had been difficult, but not impossible. After all, she'd done it before, after the death of her mother, then her father. Then again, when she'd had to fight for the job she felt she'd been born to do.

But that's what she did well. Fight for what she wanted.

And she wanted Mitchell Conner gone.

Didn't she? Her trembling limbs and pounding heart said otherwise, but she couldn't afford to indulge the weakness. Not when every ounce of her intelligence told her she'd never survive another loss.

Without allowing herself to think too much, she wrote up her article on Mitch's return. If she ran it, she'd annoy the hell out of him. She had no intention of doing so, though it had nothing to do with sparing his feelings. The most private of people, she just couldn't handle having everyone know any more sordid details of her life than they already knew.

Still, she wrote, using the activity to heal. It wasn't as easy as she'd thought, but before long she was finished describing first Mitch's strange disappearance, then his return.

She refused to dwell on the fact that she had no proof to either rebut or back up his claims. It didn't matter to her whether it was truth or fiction, she had no intention of ever running the article.

It was simply good therapy.

And when she was done, she tossed it in the trash.

Hours later Mitzy walked into Justine's office, look-ing for some proofs she needed. Everyone was long gone, but as she often did, she'd slept all day, resting off the effects of the party the night before. Now she had to write up her article and have it turned in by her 9 A.M. deadline the following morning.

And she needed the photos that went with her article; where would they be? As she circled the small, neat office her gaze skimmed over the trash . . . then back again.

Notes, tossed away? Justine never threw anything away. She must be hiding something, hopefully something really good.

Aha, she thought with triumph, scooping up Justine's discarded notepad.

"This is just too easy," she said out loud, smiling as she read her boss's aggressive and heartfelt words on Mitch's return.

Too easy, and far too irresistible.

Still smiling, Mitzy marked Justine's article ready, and called down to the print room.

"Have you started yet?" she asked, hoping. "No? Good. I have a replacement for my article." It was hard to keep from laughing. "Same length. Yep, I'll send it right down."

Mitzy pictured Justine's face when she read the article she'd meant to throw away. Hugging the pad to her chest, she beamed.

Just too much fun.

FIVE

Mitch walked into his newly acquired house and was immediately assaulted by memories. Some painful, some happy, but each one welcome.

He'd lived here until he was ten, here in this huge, warm, wonderful house. His mother, small, sweet, and loving, had been a homemaker, lavishing attention and joy on her only child. His father had been somewhat of an enigma. Mitch could hardly even remember what he'd looked like. He'd been a big man, tall and powerfully built. He'd also been unusually quiet, introverted and soft-spoken. Mitch could remember him spending long, grueling hours away, on a job that remained a mystery to this day.

Even so, he'd been a happy kid, living a good life. Playing with the other kids on the block, eating his mother's home-baked cookies, sliding down the curved oak banister . . . This house had been his home, his haven.

It was empty now, stripped of all those fond memories. It smelled musty, even though someone—probably the overzealous realtor—had at least removed the cobwebs.

How often had he promised his mother he'd buy this place back for her someday? And how often had she smiled sadly at him, telling him it didn't matter?

It *did* matter, to him.

His hands fisted in his pockets as he stood in the entry. He'd done the best he could, but it had come too late. His mother had been gone a long time now, had died of cancer a week after his high-school graduation.

Slowly he walked through the foyer, his footsteps echoing. He'd thought they'd been happy here, his mother and father and himself, but he knew now that appearances meant nothing and the young were blind. Age changed things, and age had changed his perception of those early years significantly.

He could remember the closed doors, and muted, angry voices behind them. His parents. Fighting, shouting, crying. *Over him?* It made him feel sick to think so, but he couldn't banish the thought, even now

Then one day his father had disappeared. Just like that. *Vanished*. Mitch had never heard from him again.

The boy he'd been had blamed himself; the man he was now shifted uneasily from the thought.

"It's still the same," he said into the quiet, trying to dispel the uncomfortable memories. He'd wanted the house to be light and clean. Happy the way it had seemed to him once.

He walked through the kitchen, eyed the oven and stove. From the day his father had left, his mother had stopped cooking. She'd stopped laughing too. They'd moved to an apartment that was little more than a hole in the wall, where she'd worked ten hours a day, sleeping the rest away.

Sleep hadn't come as easily for him, but rage had. He'd spent most of those years filled with it, promising vengeance on the man he felt had destroyed his mother's happiness.

Mitch had vowed this, even as he continued to blame himself for what had happened to his happy little family. He knew damn well it would have killed his mother to know how much he believed the fault to be his. That he believed his father had left because of *him*.

But by then she'd sunk so far into her own loneliness and depression, she didn't, or couldn't, notice.

Mitch had stayed angry and filled with the need for revenge for as long as he could, but the anger had eventually succumbed to sheer aloneness. He tried, desperately, to get his mother to crack the shell she'd put up around herself, to no avail.

In the end he'd been left to fend for himself, but he'd learned quickly enough. He'd gotten good at being alone, had even liked it.

Until Jussie had come into his life; sweet, caring, beautiful Jussie.

She'd reopened the heart he'd closed off. And from the day she had agreed to tutor him, he'd known . . . she was the one. She was the one who could convince him to try his hand at letting someone in. To try love, *real* love.

The kind of enduring love that would be returned, so he wouldn't have to pretend to like being alone.

But Jussie'd had her own demons to face. The loss of her parents. Surviving in a well-meaning but too-big foster family. The constant battle of keeping her brother with her. Coming up with money to go to college, as she wanted to do so badly, while keeping Devlin safe and cared for.

She had been no more ready for love than he'd been, and even less willing to accept it.

It had taken him only eight years to get her down the wedding aisle, eight glorious, laughter- and love-filled years. He'd been gone for long periods while serving in the navy, and she'd been busy with college. But while the separations had been painful, they had never once affected their closeness.

They'd grown up together, and in the process had forged a bond stronger than time.

Or so he hoped.

He could remember their wedding so clearly. Standing next to Jussie, with love and pride filling his heart. She'd looked up at him when he'd reached for her hand, love bursting from her shy smile.

Love, hope, and dreams. Because of Jussie, he'd dared to allow himself to have them once again.

In the silence, he swore and shoved his fingers through his hair as if he could scrub the memories away. He couldn't. He'd had a family with Jussie and Devlin, *the best*, and just as with his own family, he'd blown it.

Suddenly tired, Mitch leaned against the counter, staring sightlessly out the garden window. Was this how Jussie felt then, lost and deserted? Did she feel the same about his leaving her as he did about his father's desertion? It didn't matter that Mitch had never *intended* to abandon her, her feelings were the same as if he had.

How could he overcome that?

He went to sleep overwhelmed by the daunting task. But in the morning, he woke up feeling more positive. "I'm not done fighting for her," he whispered to his reflection in the mirror as he shaved. "I won't give up."

He needed to believe it would work out.

Then he read the morning *Daily News*, and Jussie's exposé—*on him*. And while he didn't know exactly which emotion was the strongest—anger, hurt, surprise, or reluctant amusement at her need to get the last word—he did know two things.

One, no matter what Jussie said, they *were* meant to be together.

And two, *he* was going to get the last word. Right before he strangled her.

Justine stayed up too late packing, preparing for the move she'd have to make all too soon. Then she slept badly, plagued by bad dreams and haunting visions, and for the first time in her life she missed the alarm clock.

Some part of her consciousness was well aware that she was dreaming, but the warm arms surrounding her, the soft, sexy voice whispering in her ear drew her deeper.

She didn't want to awaken, not when she could pretend that it was real, that Mitch really held her.

But eventually the blaring music from her radio alarm got through. So did the insistent, annoying banging.

Groaning, Justine willed all the noise away, but it kept coming. Never one to awaken easily, Justine grumbled and moaned a bit as she stumbled to the front door. She'd barely turned the lock before it burst open.

Mitch pushed past her and slammed the door shut, then pressed her back against it before she could so much as blink. He wore a dark polo shirt and snug jeans that stretched over his powerful body in a way that made her ache.

"Silly fool!" he exclaimed, giving her a good shake, hard enough that she rapped her head on the wood.

She opened her mouth to balk just as he jerked her against him, and swallowed those words whole. He devoured her mouth ruthlessly, his hands strong and impatient on her. The utter shock of it rendered her oblivious to everything but the blood bursting through her veins.

"Damn you," he said, lifting his head a fraction and blasting her with a furious stare.

She realized with horror that while his arms on her body had loosened, she'd plastered herself to his body, clinging like a vine. "The last time you kissed me like that," she managed to say shakily, pushing back from him, "was—"

"Five minutes before our wedding." He looked as dazed as she felt. "I sneaked into the church choir room where you were dressing." The fight went out of him and he sagged against her, pressing his forehead to hers. "God, what I'd give to hand you back these past years." His lifted his gaze to hers. "But I can't, Jussie, I can't. Why did you write a piece like that? Why didn't you let *me* tell you? You knew I wanted to."

"What are you talking about?"

Reaching into his back pocket, he yanked out the paper and thrust it at her.

"I wrote this." She looked at him as shock and fury filled her. "But I didn't run it."

"No?" He made a sound of scorn. "Looks like your byline to me."

Now she understood his rage. She'd refused to listen

to him, wouldn't let him tell her the story, yet as far as he believed, she had just told the entire town.

She would have been as upset as he if she weren't so absolutely furious. Without speaking, she whirled and grabbed her phone. Dialing the paper, she waited impatiently for her answer.

Once she had it, she was even more upset.

Slowly, she hung up the phone and turned to face Mitch. "Mitzy is going to die," she said conversationally.

He was still, just watching her, anger radiating from his every pore.

"I didn't plan to run that article, Mitch. I'm very sorry. I wrote it to express my feelings, then threw it away."

"Did it help?"

She caught it, the faint easing of tension from his shoulders, the light of his inherent good humor in those incredible eyes. "Not much."

"Why?"

"Because I didn't have all the facts."

"You couldn't have. There's no proof of what happened to me." His eyes narrowed when she lowered her eyes. "That's part of the problem, isn't it? You need proof of where I was. Proof I don't have."

She shrugged nonchalantly, not easy when over six feet of rough and tough, solid, angry male stared at her. A small part of her conceded his point. She might be editor now, but she was a reporter at heart. That heart came with well-honed instincts. Every one of them was screaming at her to go for it, to listen to him. That it would be worth it. That he'd tell her the truth.

Too bad the rest of her heart didn't want to hear it.

"Don't," he said thickly. His hands dove in her hair

and drew her head back. "Don't you *dare* shrug this off. You're hurt, and I understand that, better than you might think. But you know what happened to me, or you *think* you know, and you're still mad. *Why?*"

"I don't know." She looked at him, and lost her breath. The connection between them was instant, shocking. Even now, after all the pain, the powerful connection shot to life. With a single touch. With just a look. His searing gaze devoured her from her toes to the very tips of her rioting hair.

"You're not dressed." His voice sounded gruff.

Justine glanced down at herself, and felt heat flood her face. Her white nightshirt, short and sheer, hid little. Especially not the fact that she wore nothing beneath it, that she, despite herself, was unbearably aroused.

What threw a bucket of cold water on those emotions was the memory of the last time she'd worn white for him. She'd lain in that luxurious hotel suite, after their wedding, cloaked in nothing but white silk and hopes and dreams. Waiting . . . alone.

The memory of that night, and the ones that followed, was far too intense to bear. The urge to cry both overwhelmed and shamed her. She could let him tell her all of it as he wanted, let him soothe her with the words she knew he probably had. But she couldn't risk her heart and soul like that. Not again. Crossing her arms over herself, she lifted her chin. "I want you to go." Realizing how harshly she'd spoken, she added softly, "Please, Mitch."

"That's the first time you've said my name."

The stinging behind her eyes at his tender tone was going to become a flood any second. "I'm late for work, and for that I'm sorry. I'll be there."

His jaw tightened. "I don't give a damn about you being late."

"I do." This horrible, soul-destroying tension had to stop. "We have to work together, you've made certain of that."

"I did it for you," he said. "I don't know the first thing about running the *Daily News*. That's your job. Now that I'm back, I want to—"

"No," she said quickly, holding up her hand. "I don't want to know."

"Because that would mean you're getting close to me again, right?" he asked silkily. "And you don't want that. But you don't understand—"

"I *do* understand." Or she wanted to think she did. "I just . . . don't want you coming here anymore. If you need to talk to me, make it in the office."

He stared at her, clearly startled.

"I mean it." Her voice shook, but she lifted her chin firmly. "Good-bye, Mitch."

"*What?*"

"You understood me."

He snatched open the front door. Morning light spilled in, highlighting the bones in his rugged face, the tension in his body. "What I understand is you're stubborn as hell."

When the door slammed, Justine closed her eyes tight, refusing to cry. It was over. But a tear slipped past, leaving a salty track.

She'd gotten her wish. He was gone.

Again.

SIX

Mitch sat in the parking lot of the Daily News Building and punched in the sequence of numbers he'd long ago committed to memory.

"Hopkins here," said the gruff voice, bringing to mind the short, powerfully built agent who could have passed for an NFL linebacker. Instead, he'd been Mitch's only friend for the past two years, his one personal contact.

"Hopkins," Mitch said quickly, tense. "Did you find out why Jussie wasn't told about what happened to me?"

"Slipup," he admitted, sighing. "I'm sorry, Mitch. It was a bad one."

Anger and bitterness would get him nothing but clouded judgment. Or so Mitch tried to tell himself. "Terrific. I give you guys two years of my life, and in return you destroy my marriage. Thanks."

"That bad, huh?" Hopkins asked with real sympathy. "I thought she'd be thrilled. The way you went on about her, partner, I thought she was a saint."

"*Ex*-partner," Mitch corrected, to which he got a colorful reply.

Hopkins had been the first agent to approach Mitch when he'd planned to leave the SEALs. He'd also been the one to take Mitch away from his wedding-night celebration. After that, despite the fact that Hopkins was supposedly Mitch's superior, they'd become friends, mostly because Mitch had no one else.

Hopkins had saved Mitch's life more than once, and vice versa. When there'd been no one to trust but his own instincts, Hopkins had been there. When there'd been nothing but despair and heartache, Hopkins had distracted him with work and more work until Mitch could go on. And when Hopkins had lost his wife to cancer, Mitch had understood the pain better than anyone. The trust they had in each other went back only a few years, but it was stronger than time.

"Your SEAL days may be over," Hopkins conceded, "but your special-agent ones don't have to be."

They'd been through this a hundred times. A thousand. When Mitch had first disappeared into the Protection Program, he'd been left alone in a small town in Kansas, of all places. But boredom and fury had been dangerous company, and Mitch had allowed himself to be talked into working for the FBI, as Hopkins's partner. Temporarily. They'd taken on uncountable aliases and personas, cracking case after case across the globe.

Their mutual desperation and despair had made them invincible.

"I'm through, Hopkins," Mitch said with no regret. "I have to be."

"You sure?"

Mitch thought of Jussie, and the life he hoped to have with her. "I've never been so sure of anything in all my life."

He'd finagled the parking spot right next to hers, Justine discovered a short time later. It came as a shock, seeing the convertible that looked so like his old one, only this car had been completely cherried out.

It wasn't the one from their youth, but it was close enough to have her squirming with the memories.

Mitch had taught her to drive in that car, among other things. Heat flooded her face as she remembered some of those *other* things now, and despite the cold morning breeze, she felt hot. Unable to help herself, she glanced at the backseat, remembering more than a few dark nights. Long, drugging kisses. Steamy embraces that had led to fumbling for leg room. Muffled laughter, and then more fumbling . . . *God.*

She closed her eyes and tried for calm, but it was nowhere to be found. Nowhere.

Maybe it was someone else's car, she thought hopefully, but she knew better. No one at the paper could afford such a car—except her *very*-soon-to-be ex-husband.

She kept thinking that, she realized, but she hadn't done a thing about it. She'd call a lawyer today.

Ignoring the strange *ping* in her insides, she walked briskly toward the building, thinking about work. About how she was going to cheerfully chew out Mitzy—right before she fired her for rifling through her office and running that article behind her back.

She also had new information from her brother's

anonymous source, providing her with info about the mayor and his suspiciously well-endowed funds. Seemed the man might be at it again, which would make great copy. Work should have cheered her.

But her stomach tightened suddenly as a dark blue sedan drove sedately past her. Too sedately. Unreasonable fear rose up.

The windows were tinted. She shuddered in the warm sun. "I've got to stop watching *The X-Files*," she muttered, realizing she needed to relax a little. Still, she nearly fell over at the unexpected soft voice from behind her.

"Well, look what the cat dragged in."

Justine whirled, and faced a smug-looking Mitzy. Biting back her temper, she smiled. "Just the woman I wanted to see. You're fired."

Mitzy's eyes widened innocently. "Whatever for?"

"You know damn well what for. As an employee here, you're trusted automatically. That trust was hopelessly destroyed this morning."

"Because I ran the article you didn't have the guts to run?"

"Because you violated my privacy. Because you went against company policy. Because you think this is funny, damn you."

"You shouldn't fire me. I'm greatly loved." Mitzy grinned confidently. "It'll be trouble for you."

Justine knew that of course, just as she knew she couldn't afford more trouble. "Suspended then. You've got two weeks off."

"Your readers will scream."

"Which is the only thing saving your job."

Mitzy smoothed down her skintight lime-colored suit and shrugged. "I was wondering what you thought of the party the other night. Your temper tells me everything I need to know."

"What do you want, Mitzy?" Justine asked wearily.

"Did you know I'm up for the Woman of the Year award?"

Justine crossed her arms and studied the employee she knew all too well. "Did you nominate yourself?"

"Hey, that award is given for excellence in community service. I've been quite the little giver this year." Uninsulted, Mitzy checked her hair. "I've made sure of it."

"Nothing like a do-gooder." It bothered Justine how much of the money Mitzy collected was wasted on her huge, lavish fund-raisers. She'd prefer to see one hundred percent go back to each particular charity, but to someone like Mitzy, the fun was in the event itself, and no expense could be spared.

Too bad it wasn't Mitzy's own money, or her father's.

"You still have to win the majority of votes," Justine pointed out. "That's not too likely."

"Of course it is, especially since Daddy's doing so well."

"According to the papers, that's debatable."

Mitzy laughed and gave Justine an insulting once-over. She wrinkled her nose as if finding Justine's quietly understated business attire lacking. "So is it true, Justine? Is *he* really back for good?"

"Who?"

"Don't be coy." Mitzy cocked an eyebrow. "That's *my* job."

Tired of games, Justine looked away. Off to the right was an open courtyard, where employees often went on break or to gossip. It was filled now, as people changed shifts. On the far side stood Devlin and Mitch, heads bent as if deep in discussion.

They were both striking, but maturity and sheer presence drew the eye directly to Mitch. His dark hair was lit by the bright sun, and even from a distance, his eyes sparkled. Suddenly he threw back his head and laughed, and the sight of the man and the pleasure in his voice had Justine's insides tingling in unwanted desire.

"God, he's something," Mitzy said under her breath.

"He's mine," Justine said mildly, gently tapping the other woman's gaping chin. "Get a napkin; you're drooling."

Later, Justine wondered what had gotten into her. *He's mine?* Good Lord, she'd sounded so possessive.

It took her a few minutes to wind her way to her office because she stopped in different departments to check on the day's progress. But eventually she entered her office, and made yet another unwelcome discovery.

Mitchell Conner had claimed the office right next to hers.

Since the wall between the two rooms was glass, and since only *his* side had mini-blinds on them—which he'd pulled up—she had a full, unwelcome view of him.

And he of her.

Sprawled out in his chair, with his impossibly long legs up on his desk and his feet crossed, Mitch looked the picture of a relaxed man. But his white, long-sleeved shirt stretched taut over equally taut shoulders, and the broad callused hands that rested on his flat stomach were clenched tight. So was his jaw.

He was talking to Anne, her secretary, and through the glass she could just barely hear their muted voices. There was laughter in his, despite his clear tension. But when he caught a glimpse of Justine, that laughter vanished.

Anne followed his gaze, gave Justine a knowing little smile, then left the room.

For a few seconds neither Justine nor Mitch moved, hopelessly pinned in the moment. His gaze was piercing, intense, yet for the life of her, she couldn't look away.

Her phone rang suddenly into the silence, and she leaped for it, grateful for the diversion. But it was a momentary one, since her caller hung up with a rude click in her ear.

After that, Justine managed to avoid Mitch for a while, busy with her endless responsibilities. But her phone drove her crazy. She got three more hang-ups in a row, all within an hour. Often after a particularly unpopular piece in the paper, they were besieged with complaints. She'd have to check yesterday's paper and see which group they could have annoyed this time.

She got one last call—heavy breathing, followed immediately by a thick, raspy voice saying, "I'm watching you."

Justine hung up with a quick shudder. In her business, crank calls weren't so unusual, but *this* was a new one. She tried to use the distraction to forget her other, bigger problem.

But it was difficult to ignore a man who could gain her attention without saying a word. For wherever she went, she saw Mitch. Felt him.

In the print room, where she'd wandered down after learning the air-conditioning vents had given out, she discovered a summer climate right in the middle of winter. They'd shut down the computers so they wouldn't overheat, and as time dragged on she became worried about the next day's edition.

The heat had her hair sticking to her face. She glanced up at one point from a conversation with Max, the printer, to find Mitch standing at the entrance. He was hot, too, given the way his shirt clung to every inch of his broad shoulders and back, outlining sinew and bone structure that made her mouth water.

Ciji, one of the printers, happened by. From somewhere, the young woman had procured a squirt bottle, and had it hooked to the belt of her skirt. Laughing, she sprayed first her face, then after a brief hesitation in which she checked Mitch out from beneath coy lashes, she sprayed his as well.

His laughter rang out.

Inexplicably annoyed, Justine looked away, hastening to finish her business so she could go back to her cool office and indulge her need to sulk.

But a minute later, unable to help herself, she turned back. Mitch, alone now, looked right back, leaving her hopelessly flustered. Good Lord, but he was hot, wet, and gorgeous. And looking good enough to eat. She bit her tongue rather than have it fall out, and fanned her face wildly with the papers in her hand.

Slowly, he approached her, and all she could do was watch, incapable of escaping because her feet seemed to have suddenly glued themselves to the floor.

"Hi," he said.

She had to smile, if for no other reason than that it

felt just a bit absurd to be constantly around him after so long. "Hi back. I guess."

His crooked smile kept hers in place as he swiped at his face. "Too bad this newspaper life isn't for me. Working here wouldn't be too bad." He grinned at her wickedly and her heart did a slow roll in her chest. "The boss lady is a looker."

She flushed and he laughed.

"The redheaded curse," he said with mock sympathy. "Poor Jus. If your eyes don't tell me your mood, your face sure will." He reached out with a long finger and stroked a fire-hot cheek. "It's what makes you so appealing, you know. That inability to be anything but brutally honest." His eyes sobered. "The truth is everything. I wish you'd listen to it."

She swallowed, dropped her gaze to her feet. "I'm . . . not ready, Mitch."

"I know. And though I hate it, I do understand. Just remember this, Jussie, I never meant to leave you."

He went silent a moment, and she expected him to push, to probe. But he didn't, and that only confused her all the more.

He looked around them. "It's nice to see this. To watch you do the job you were born for. You're good at it."

The compliment, as most did, embarrassed her. "It practically runs itself."

"It takes skill. And you've got it."

"No," she said solemnly, her strange joy at being near him fading. "If I had it, *you* wouldn't be writing the checks."

"Jussie—"

"No." She shook her head. "It's not your fault.

And . . ." That was *her* being paged on the intercom, thank God. "And I've got to go."

She felt his gaze heat her back as she walked away. Her limbs actually quivered, but she kept going. She had to work.

It was all she had left.

Justine's office was cool enough, wonderfully so. The only problem: Having Mitch in the next room sort of dissipated the good effects. It was the dead of winter, but with the man this close, it might as well have been summer.

She couldn't change her body's reaction to him, but she *could* pretend it wasn't a problem.

With her hair plastered to the back of her neck and her dress sticking to her spine, she worked, refusing to do what she wanted to do most—glance over at Mitch.

Several times she caught herself just in time. *She wouldn't look, she wouldn't.*

But she did, and found that she couldn't turn away from the greenest, deepest gaze she'd ever seen. Then he grinned and she quickly looked away.

Even through the glass, she had no trouble hearing Mitch's low, amused laugh. *Terrific.* While this intense, anticipatory heat between the two of them was slowly strangling her, *he* apparently thrived on it.

An hour later, when she entered a crowded elevator trying to get up to copy editing two floors above, she froze as the doors shut.

It wasn't the sudden, awkward silence that tipped her off. Nor the fact that all eyes shifted unerringly to her.

Ten people in that damned elevator. Yet she felt a

tingling, an awareness that could be attributed to just one person. Slowly, she turned . . . and bumped into her friend Jack.

He smiled at her warmly, but she could manage only a weak one in return. Behind him, tall enough that she could clearly see his face over Jack, stood Mitch. He no longer looked amused, and before she could remember she didn't care, she wondered what had happened to put that scowl on his face.

Oblivious, Jack tugged on a loose strand of her hair. "I won."

"Excuse me?" she stammered, cursing her luck for stepping onto this elevator, now, here, with *him*.

"Our bet?" Jack said, still grinning. "Kings lost, I win."

"Oh." Just two days ago her life had been normal enough that she had been joking around with Jack.

"You owe me lunch," he said. "But I'd be willing to roll it over into the next bet if you'll throw in a movie and popcorn on the next loss."

They'd been doing this for the last few years. Betting on games. Justine won more often than not. And obviously, Jack was expecting her usual bantering. "Okay," was all the answer she could muster, with Mitch's searing gaze on hers.

"*Okay?*" Jack repeated with a surprised laugh. "Last time you lost you ranted and raved for an hour, and now just okay?" He shook his head and pretended to check her for a temperature. "You sick?"

No, but she had a feeling Jack was going to be if he kept his hands on her. Mitch looked positively furious. Jack's hands were smooth, practiced. They lingered.

And she felt nothing, though she knew it was her lack, not Jack's. Any woman with a set of eyes would be falling all over herself for his attentions. He was good-looking, kind, sophisticated. Romantic.

But she couldn't keep her eyes off Mitch.

No one else said a word.

"We've got to get together on those figures, sweetie," Jack said. "Year end is only days away."

Slowly, Mitch quirked an eyebrow. "Sweetie?" he mouthed, his gaze boring right through her. He'd once been patient to a fault, and mild-tempered, despite his strenuous and demanding occupation. But bad attitude screamed from him now.

"Yes, Jack," she said quickly, wondering why the elevator wouldn't hurry, why no one else in the car spoke. "This afternoon. My office—" she started to say, remembered the glass wall would reveal Mitch watching, and changed her mind. "On second thought, *your* office would be . . . more convenient."

Jack grinned at that. "Great. But I'm busy until five-thirty."

Mitch frowned. His eyes darkened. But still he waited, with a glimmer of his old patience, obviously sure she'd say something.

She didn't.

"We'll order in takeout," Jack said, maybe not so oblivious after all.

Either way, he had a death wish, for Mitch turned a mottled sort of red. The elevator slowed.

"Excuse me," Mitch said roughly, pushing past Jack. Ignoring him, he turned the full blast of his heavy stare on Justine. "That won't work."

She had to lick her suddenly dry lips. "Why?"

Her heart thudded heavily at the way his gaze turned hungry and hot at the movement. "You're busy tonight," he murmured, still looking at her mouth. "Quite busy."

"Yes," Jack agreed evenly. "Working on the books."

"Check again," Mitch suggested, a barely leashed violence seeping from every syllable.

A scene. Right here in the elevator. Wouldn't that just cap her day off nicely? "Won't be necessary," she said quickly just as the elevator stopped. "I'm not busy."

"Chinese or pizza?" Jack asked. He was still smiling, but his body had gone tense with the suggestion of trouble.

The elevator doors slid open, the audible sigh of relief from the others the only sound to be heard. Justine nearly ran off, but forced herself to remain calm as everyone scrambled to get as far away as possible.

Jack hesitated, looking at her in a way that told her he wasn't budging, unless she wanted him to. "Justine?"

She'd never been so aware of anyone in her life as she was of Mitch at that moment. He stood there, silent, just watching her. Waiting. He let his gaze skim over her, lingering at her mouth, which parted of its own accord. She had to do something, and quickly. It was bad enough Jack was watching, but it was worse, much worse, that her heart was hammering out of control because of a *look*. "I'll get back to you, Jack. Thanks."

He nodded slowly, then glanced at Mitch. An unspoken conversation went on without her, then Jack walked away.

She turned to do the same.

"Justine."

Her full name. When was the last time he'd used it like that, in that cool tone? "Yes?"

"I need a moment of your time," he said firmly, cutting off her polite refusal.

She glared at him.

He glared back. Then his shoulders suddenly slumped. "You're driving me crazy," he said miserably. "Absolutely certifiably crazy."

An unwilling smile tugged at her lips before she could stop it. "It's mutual, then."

"Sick as this sounds," he murmured, "somehow that makes me feel better."

"Great. Glad I could help."

Cocking his head, his gaze once again took a leisurely tour of her, leaving her with the ridiculous urge to cover herself, though she was fully clothed in a blouse and skirt.

"Stop that," she hissed, glancing self-consciously around.

"I've dreamed about looking at you for so long, I can't possibly stop. I may never get my fill again."

The low, husky voice unnerved her. So did the way her breasts tightened and heat pooled between her legs. He noticed, she thought with panic as his eyes settled on her pebbled nipples where they poked against the material of her blouse.

"Come out with me tonight," he said softly, stepping closer.

"W-what? Why?"

"We have things to discuss. See me tonight." His eyes softened as he took one more step, bringing them within inches of each other. "We need to talk. We need to be alone. Let's go out and do both."

"As in a . . . date?"

He smiled that endearing grin, and damn her heart, it fluttered. "Yeah," he said. "As in a date."

"I—well, I don't—"

"Scared?"

She lifted her chin at that. "Of course not! I just have work to do, that's all."

He shook his head and leaned close enough that she could smell that unique scent that was his alone. "I think you're afraid of me, afraid of what I make you feel."

"That's absurd." But her voice shook, betraying her. "And I don't have time for dates."

"Not even with your husband?"

"You're not my husband—"

"Aren't I?" He paused. "Jussie, you know I didn't leave you on purpose. That I—"

"Devlin told me." In a gesture she recognized as childish and defensive, she crossed her arms over her chest. "He told me what happened."

"But you didn't let him finish, I imagine," he guessed correctly. "You were never the patient one. God knows how you managed to build a career as a reporter."

"He told me enough."

"No," he disagreed. "He didn't. If he had, we wouldn't be doing this asinine thing where we stare stupidly at each other, burning and yearning. We'd be home. In *bed*," he said bluntly.

Her body tingled again. And because it did, she resisted him with everything she had. "I can't believe how cocky you are. Coming back here after all this time and—"

"That's what this boils down to, your hurt and anger over my disappearance. You think I did this on purpose, despite me telling you otherwise." He shook his head, lowered his voice until she had to lean even closer to hear him. She couldn't miss the pain in it. "I know what it's like to be left, Jussie. I know. It hurts like hell, tears a hole in your soul. I can help heal it.

Unreasonable fear welled. "No."

"Please."

The anguish in his voice shamed her, even as she shook her head. She imagined what he'd been through had been horrifying. But a little part of her wanted to believe he could have taken her with him, or that he could have contacted her somehow. It made it easier to hold on to the hurt and to dismiss the way she'd caved in the instant he'd touched her.

"You have to hear it all before you decide," he said a little roughly. "Then, maybe, you can make such a rash decision."

Justine didn't think she was ready to hear it all, but it didn't matter much what she thought, because Mitch took her hand and led her down the hall. "Where are we—"

He opened the door to the stairwell and tugged her in. When the heavy steel door shut, the busy sounds of the newsroom behind them faded away. "We're taking the stairs. It seems to be more private than the elevator. As I was saying . . ." He started down the stairs, pulling her along with a grip of steel. "About what happened to us, about what's going to happen—"

"I don't want to hear it," she said, trying to pull her wrist free.

Fury welled in him at her stubbornness, but Mitch bit it back. Not easy when he'd lived the last two years as he had in order to keep her safe, not easy when she resented him for it. Especially when he so understood that resentment. "You're going to hear it."

"No. I—"

"Be quiet, Jussie," he managed to say quite calmly. Calmness was a particular talent of his, or had been until Jussie had come back into his life.

"Let go of me."

He didn't. All patience had evaporated. At the next stairwell, he opened the door. Without a word, he pulled her down a surprisingly quiet hallway, searching for what he needed. "Why is it so quiet in here?"

"These offices aren't used right now."

"Perfect." He opened a door at random, discovered exactly what he'd been hoping for, and pushed her inside. From the outside, he popped a chair under the handle, wedging it tightly. Then he leaned against the door and waited.

"What?" came her confused voice. She knocked on the door. "Hey!"

He took a deep breath and remained silent.

"This is a storage closet!" The handle near his hip was tested lightly, then with much more force. "Mitch? Let me out!"

He smiled grimly and waited some more.

"Mitch!"

"Yeah. I'm right here."

"What the hell's going on?" she demanded. "You . . . locked me in?"

"Hmm, I just used a chair. We're having a little problem with trust here, Jussie."

"Wait." He heard a thunk, as if she'd dropped her forehead to the door. "You've locked me in a storage closet?"

"That's right. Ready to listen yet?"

SEVEN

"I can't believe this!" came Jussie's muffled voice.

From the outside of the locked storage closet, Mitch prepared himself for the unavoidable battle and pressed his back to the door. "Believe it, baby. I locked you in. Should have done it yesterday." He'd wanted to, but had wanted even more to have her listen willingly.

The ensuing silence was filled with seething rage. "Mitch," she said in a quietly fulminating voice. "I want out. Now."

"Hmm." He leaned back and stroked his chin. "Yes, nice use of my name, which I appreciate, by the way. Especially since you've done your best to call me *nothing* for two days. But I'd really love to hear you call me *husband*."

"Open this door, damn you."

"Can't."

"I'll scream."

He couldn't help it, he suddenly grinned as he remembered his sweet, quiet Jussie was indeed a screamer.

If she wanted to, she could blow the lid off the building. "Feel free."

Nothing.

His grin faded. "I didn't leave you, Jussie. My heart's been with you this entire time. I need you to believe that."

More silence.

"I witnessed something I wasn't supposed to." He was determined to tell her the truth, and equally determined for her to understand. "The day before our wedding, at a meeting where I'd just refused to work for the government—again—another agent and I witnessed a crime. We did the law-abiding thing, only to discover the law doesn't always work." Yes, he was still quite bitter, he discovered. "Especially since the crime had been committed by an insider. He was on the take, Jussie. A real bad guy. The agent I was with was killed over it."

"Mitch, let me out."

"I was tagged, Jussie. Do you know what that means?"

"I—"

"I was earmarked to die. Just like the other guy." He heard the soft gasp and took heart. "I didn't know that, of course. Not until directly after our wedding. The feds took me away." And after extracting a promise to see the case through, they'd made him stay away from her. "They kept me safe. I went immediately into the Protection Program."

There was a long moment of silence. "And you disappeared."

"Yes." He turned to face the door, then put his palms on it, wishing he was touching her face. "I had to, for your sake, and Devlin's. You two were all I cared about, and with me around, you would have been in grave danger."

"You never even contacted me."

God, the wealth of hurt in her voice twisted his gut. "I couldn't. It would have put you at risk. But the feds were supposed to. They promised to explain, to tell you what had happened, and I believed they had done so." All the old anger surged back. "There was a mix-up." Was it safe to let her out? Would she listen to the rest?

"Why didn't you take me with you?"

She would have come. He knew that now, but at the time all he could think was that she'd resent being taken from her life. Forced to change names, live far away. She'd have no paper to run. No Devlin, unless he had wanted to come as well. But the FBI had half convinced him it would be too many leaks, too many chances.

And he'd had no idea he would have to be gone so long. No idea he would be held to a promise made in the heat of danger and intrigue to see justice done. "It's rough, Jussie. An awful life. A new name, new identity. I never stayed in one place for long. You would have hated it."

"Then you're the one who's clueless," she whispered, emotion thickening her voice.

He thought his heart had broken long ago, but he was wrong. "Jussie, I'm sorry."

"I tried to find you."

She said it casually, but he knew better. To Jussie, such a statement was a huge admission of feeling. "I—"

"Let me out," she said suddenly, and he straightened, narrowing his eyes on the door as if he could see through it. "Not yet. You've forgotten how much we meant to each other. Which drives me crazy, but in spite of myself, I understand."

"No, you don't."

"Yes," he said softly. "I do. When my father left, my mother made excuses for him. Said he had to go, had to be free. It wasn't anyone's fault, he just had to go."

A soft sound of regret came from the closet. "Mitch."

"I hated him, Jussie. With all my heart. It kills me that you feel the same."

"I don't . . . hate you."

"I want to go back to where we were."

"There's no going back." She rattled the handle. "Let me out."

He turned and again put his back to the door, tipping his head up to study the ceiling. Images from his mind played across it like a movie. Jussie. She'd been a solemn young woman when he'd first met her, and he'd had to whittle away at her resolve to keep her world from being just work, school, and Devlin. But Mitch was and always had been a survivor, just like them, and just as alone as they were. He'd fit into their lives, and they into his.

They'd been his family, Justine and Devlin, and he loved them both. He could remember teaching them to ease up on the seriousness, just as they'd taught him how to be loyal. More images came now, faster and more vivid. Jussie laughing at some silly joke he'd made, her long, glorious hair blowing as he sped them down the highway in his car. The look on her face when he'd kissed her for the first time, shock mixed with bewildered pleasure.

And he'd never forget the last time he'd seen her before his disappearance, on their wedding day.

Now he was back to ground zero with her, resorting to locking her in a closet to get her full attention. Well, that was fitting enough, he thought wryly. It had taken him years to earn her trust the first time. He could expect it to take more than two days the second time around.

"We were so young, so ignorant, weren't we? So certain of ourselves," he said with a fond smile.

"One of us is still pretty certain of himself," Justine said, but her voice had lost some of its venom. "Let me out, Mitch."

She sounded tired. Confused. He longed to do as she wished, but this was too important. "Jussie," he said, "after our reception, we went to the hotel. I left you to go get ice for the champagne. Do you remember?"

A bitter laugh sounded. "I seem to remember that, yes." Her voice tightened, stretched, but didn't waver. "You didn't come back. I thought something had happened to you, something horrible. The police tried to help. . . ." He heard her ragged draw of breath. "They were so attentive—at first."

He spoke carefully, because the barely controlled emotion in her voice tore at him. "What do you mean, at first?"

"They decided that you'd left me. You know, on purpose."

His hands fisted. His superiors had promised to take care of that too. Hopkins had assured him they had, and Mitch had believed it because he'd needed to know she'd been taken care of, that she hadn't blamed herself. Or him. *Damn them.* "Jussie—"

"Somehow it leaked to the press, and . . ."

She trailed off, while his fingers pressed into the door. He'd left, and she'd been alone to deal with the humiliation. Apologies weren't going to cut it, not by a long shot. "But now you know it wasn't because I'd decided I didn't want to be married," he said gently, moving aside the chair and turning the handle because he had to see her. "Back away from the door, baby."

"I want out."

"Not yet, not until we finish this." He entered the closet and shut the door behind him, blinking his eyes uselessly in the absolute darkness. "Where are you?" he asked, then grunted when he backed painfully into a steel shelving unit. Turning, he reached out and felt for her, realizing by her surprised squeak that he'd just gotten a warm handful of breast. He grinned. "Sorry."

"Hmmph."

Her snootiness reminded him of her stubbornness, which in turn reminded him of why he'd had to snag her in here in the first place. Feeling for her shoulders, he took them in his hands. "Two FBI agents stopped me in the hotel hallway, *made* me go with them."

"Uh-huh," she said sardonically, and he felt her hands on him, running up his arms, testing, squeezing. "You're telling me a big guy like you, powerfully built as you are, was *made* to do something against his will?"

"They had some information," he said, cupping her face to make sure she was at least facing him, paying attention. "And guns."

Despite her mock indifference, Justine was hanging

on every word. After two years she'd gotten used to the fact that Mitch had apparently disappeared into thin air, and that the entire town had considered her "dumped." She'd allowed herself to grieve and go on.

But now the realization that he'd been made to leave against his will had started to set in, and she didn't know how she felt.

His voice reached her in the dark. "I *had* to leave, Jussie, because you were going to get tagged, too, if I didn't. Maybe Devlin as well."

"So you left to protect me. Us."

"Yes."

She could tell there was more, something he wasn't saying. She knew him well enough to realize that whatever it was, whatever he was keeping to himself, she wouldn't like it. She was thankful for the dark because she had to think, and she couldn't possibly do that with his intense green gaze on her. It was difficult enough with his hands framing her face.

"Before you ask," he said, "yes, while I was gone I was a special agent. For a while."

"A while?"

"I hated it," he admitted quietly. "I spent those years being anyone other than myself, sometimes changing identities daily. Always moving." He drew a ragged breath. "Those days are over. For good. I want to work for myself, I always have."

She knew that, and it relieved her to learn he was no longer required, or committed, to work for the government—not that it *should* matter to her. "What happened to the agent you saw on the take?"

He hesitated. "He was lost."

"Lost—you mean—"

"Yeah. Dead." He sighed and ran his hands down her arms until their fingers linked. Unwittingly, she clung to him, taking comfort from the sudden chill that had seized her.

"Jussie, the guy took bribes, then turned in his own colleagues and friends for money. He turned up dead, but we don't know why or who."

"We?"

"I worked with another agent. Hopkins. After they took me, and explained . . . we made a deal. I would go underground, and they'd make sure you were safe."

"What else? There's something else." She felt his hesitation, sensed his anger. Horrified, she shook her head, even knowing he couldn't see her. "No. No, they didn't. Tell me they didn't put a price on that protection."

"Just my freedom," he admitted hoarsely. "If I did this, and saw the case through, they'd let me out. They'd stop trying to bully me into staying."

"They made you pay for your freedom with two years of your life?"

He said nothing and her heart ached. He'd promised. He'd stayed away, for *her*.

She could feel the wheels of her investigative mind whirling. In any case, it was far easier to discuss the bizarre events that had led to his disappearance instead of how she felt about it. "What was this agent working on, the one who died mysteriously?"

"It involved kickbacks from a huge corporation. With such big money involved, the temptation got to be too much for him. He got greedy."

The thought that came next had her pulling her

hands out of his and backing as far away as the small, dark space allowed. "Maybe there's still a threat."

"No."

"But you can't be sure, can you? Maybe you came back just to protect me."

"Jussie—"

"No. Wait." Her thoughts raced as she slapped a hand up, blocking his body from pressing closer to hers. Beneath her hand, his chest felt solid. His heartbeat was steady and strong, and on their own, her fingers spread, touching all she could. God, she ached. "You came back for me." But not out of a sense of any undying love, as a small part of her had been hoping. "Out of a sense of duty."

"No." He caught her close again, ignoring her attempts to stay free. In the cramped space, they had little room to maneuver. "I came back because of this." He brought his lips to hers.

Her initial struggle died on a moan. She couldn't help it, the passion she tasted was no less volatile than the passion she felt. Her hands gripped his tense shoulders as his dragged her head back, roughly, possessively, angling for better access. A sudden wildness overcame both of them then, primitive, almost brutal, making the years of waiting, needing, yearning seem like nothing.

They broke apart, gasping for air, but Justine hadn't gotten enough, felt she could never get enough of his strong, built, and oh, so aroused body. She spread open-mouthed kisses along his tight jaw, then feeling a little savage, she bit his ear.

He moaned her name, his mouth racing over her face and throat. "Touch me," he muttered. "I'll go crazy if you don't, I've waited so long." He backed her to a table, lifted her, and lost to reason, she wrapped her legs around his waist, bringing their bodies flush together.

"More," he said, his voice muffled since his mouth was filled with her flesh. He slid his hips against hers, making her vibrantly aware of just how much he wanted her. "Jussie, more."

Mitch lost himself in her, but still it wasn't enough, could never be enough. As if starving, his hands raced over her tight, hot body. He heard her choke out his name when he tugged her blouse open and cupped her breasts in his palms. This, he thought. This was what he'd needed.

"God, you're sweet," he whispered. On a frustrated oath, he shifted her, shoving who knew what to the floor so that he could lay her back on the table. Then she was beneath him, her body moving, twisting under his, tormenting him into tasting.

He suckled and she arched, her fingers digging hard into his arms. "Please," she gasped.

He could hear the whimper, the bewildered confusion in her voice, and it fueled his fire, his desperation. Greedily, he took more.

"Mitch, please." She held on tight and rocked against him.

He bumped his head on the shelf above them, and swearing, he stood upright with her in his arms. Mindless as animals, they dragged each other to the floor. Justine reared up to rip at his shirt, yanking at the buttons as she muttered something about skin to skin. Mitch helped her, then knelt between her legs, ready to ravage.

The knock at the door startled them both into frozen statues, but only for a second, because what was about to happen flashed before Mitch's eyes. With lightning speed, he jerked upright and pressed his back to the door, just as the handle twisted at his hip.

He held his breath, and from the floor, where he knew Jussie still lay, came utter, panicked silence.

"Hello?" someone called, working the handle to no avail, thanks to Mitch's strength. "Anyone in there?"

He could practically taste Jussie's terror at being caught in this situation. Guilt swamped him for putting her in it in the first place. He could see the headlines now: MILLER AND HUSBAND, CAUGHT CONSUMMATING MAR- RIAGE IN STORAGE CLOSET.

"Damn thing's stuck," someone muttered with dis- gust, trying the handle one last time.

Finally, footsteps faded away, leaving a tense silence. Then came Jussie's shaken, released breath.

Mitch had surfaced abruptly, but he still had to shake his head to clear it. Gulping in air, he stared down into the darkness to make out the faint outline of her stiff body. Her blouse had been pushed, by him, off her shoulders, and was open to the waist. Her skirt rode high up on her thighs. One shoe had been kicked off.

He'd nearly mauled her like a reckless, sex-starved teen.

Mouth grim, body uncomfortably hard and hot, he reached down and pulled her to her feet. "Jussie," he whispered with regret, tugging her clothes back into place. God, he'd nearly taken her right there. Their first time in two years, and he'd . . . he couldn't even think about it. She deserved candles, soft music, sweet words, and hours and hours of loving.

Instead she'd gotten a cold concrete floor against her

back, fast, desperate hands, and an icy darkness. He reached for her and received a shove that surprised him into falling back against the door.

"Hands off," she demanded quite clearly, though her voice shook. She jerked away when he tried again. "Don't—don't touch me."

"I'm sorry," he said, which even to his own ears sounded hopelessly inadequate.

"Fine. You're sorry." She jerked her skirt down, whirled around, fumbling with her hands until she located her shoe. "Just keep your hands off me."

"Fine," he said, struggling to hold on to pride and composure while he buttoned his own shirt. He was missing two buttons, who knew where they were. "But that'd be an easier promise to keep if this were all one-sided."

"Move out of my way."

He blocked her path easily. "We didn't finish."

She choked out a laugh. "Oh, we finished. Believe me, we finished."

"I meant *talking*," he said tightly.

"I'm done talking." She slid under his arm and reached the door.

But he held it closed. "I'm not going to disappear again."

"A girl can hope."

"Dammit, will you stop?" He gave her a little shake. "You're basing your emotions on what you thought I'd done to you. Can't you see that? *I didn't leave you on purpose.*"

"You were still gone." Unexpectedly, she sagged, dropping her head to his chest. "I'm sorry," she whispered. "I'm more mad at myself right now than anything. I can't believe that I let you—that you—oh, God. Never mind." She lifted her head. "I need to think, Mitch. You're going to have to understand that much."

"I can do that," he promised her, and it gave Justine little satisfaction to hear the gruff emotion, the concern in his voice. "But let me know how it goes or I'll drag you back in here."

"Fine." Maybe she would. Maybe she wouldn't. She certainly didn't have to make it easy for the man who could melt her resolve with just a slanted look. She'd lost both her parents, raised her brother, fought for a job she loved, and suffered the humiliation of a very public bankruptcy, not to mention her husband's disappearance. Certainly she could handle a few days of introspection.

It was being watched by the sexiest man alive that terrified her. "You've made it clear. We have some thinking to do, *then* some talking." She jabbed at his chest. "But call someone else when you want to make out in a damn closet."

Grabbing her upper arms, he waited until her wild eyes met his. "You're important to me, Jussie. Hell," he said with a harsh laugh. "For most of my life, you've been all I had. And I *know* it was the same for you, dammit, don't you dare try to deny that. You, me, and Devlin, we were a unit. We stuck together, no matter what. Even with the odds against us, even with everyone in town wondering how long before we all got into trouble, we made it. Even when we were just kids, too young to know what we had. In all that time, for all those years, we were never anything but brutally honest. Unwaveringly loyal."

"And you want that back."

"God, yes." One hand cupped the back of her neck. "More than anything. But I want *you* to want it too."

She closed her eyes when his fingers brushed over the sensitive skin beneath her hair. "I don't know what I want."

"I can't be patient about this. I've tried, but I just can't."

"You don't have a choice," she whispered.

With that, she shoved open the door and ran down the hallway out of sight. She was gone before he could tell her that he wouldn't let her throw it all away.

He was here because he loved her, and he wanted a shot at making their marriage real.

If she were being honest, he thought, she'd admit she already knew all that. And one of these days she was going to admit she wanted the same thing.

Somehow, Justine managed to work the day through. Her hair, which had earlier been nice and neat, had gone wild. Curly, unruly strands flew everywhere. Her skirt had a suspicious-looking ink stain on the hip, and since she seemed to remember the uncomfortable length of a pen beneath her in the storage closet, her mood darkened considerably. Her nylons had a run, probably from when she'd wantonly spread herself on the floor for Mitch's pleasure.

Unbelievable!

He'd touched her and she'd completely lost herself. It wouldn't, couldn't, happen again. But just the thought had her legs trembling, so she sat at her desk and forced the memory from her mind as she tried to get some work done.

She was successful, until she got three more hang-ups in a row, then that low raspy voice telling her to "back off."

Back off what? More unnerved than she wanted to admit, she flipped through the last week of the *Daily News*, but the only truly controversial subject had been the mayor. Was the voice referring to the article she'd written in today's edition? The one where she cited proof—thanks to her source—that he'd accepted money from Q-Vac, a huge corporation on the coast, the one he'd sworn he'd had no contact with? The same corporation which, by a strange coincidence, opposed several antipollution laws that Mayor Thompson suddenly opposed as well?

She didn't know, but hoped the crank calls were just that—cranks.

Encouraged by Mitch's continued absence from his office, she worked late. Both Devlin and Jack had tried to get her to leave with them, but she'd needed to throw herself into something constructive.

Night had fallen by the time she left the building, and the lot was uncomfortably dark. With no moon, the black, wintry night seemed . . . spooky.

Even her own footsteps unnerved her, so she sped up until she was nearly running.

An unexpected rustling stopped her cold.

"Are you crazy, or do you just have a death wish?" an angry voice demanded as a figure stepped in front of her.

"Mitch!" Heart in her throat, Justine put a hand on her chest. "Don't *ever* do that again."

He pushed away from the brick wall he'd been leaning on and grabbed her arm. "You're getting an abnormal amount of hang-up calls, yet you work until you're the only one in the building, then race across a deserted, dark parking lot? Real smart, Jussie."

"How did you know about the calls?"

His smile didn't reach his eyes. "Well, my lovely wife, seems your staff just can't do enough to help our marriage along. Anne loves to talk about you."

Betrayed! If Anne hadn't been with Justine since forever, if Justine didn't care for her so much . . . oh, who was she kidding? It wasn't Anne's fault Justine suddenly found herself in this predicament.

At her car, Mitch waited with an outstretched palm until she dropped her keys into it with a noise of disgust. She'd been on her own for two years, yet after two days back in her life he was acting like a possessive . . . husband. "I've been opening my own doors for a while now."

Silently, he unlocked the door, jerked it open, and pushed her into the driver's seat.

Straightening, he glared at her while she put on her seat belt. "See that car?" He pointed to the dark blue sedan she'd noticed before. "It's going to follow you home. Don't lose it."

"Why?"

"Why?" he asked incredulously. "I want you safe, dammit."

She felt a surge of disappointment that it wouldn't be Mitch who would follow her, then ruthlessly squelched it. She didn't want to see him anyway. "I've seen that car before."

"You couldn't have. I just called Hopkins, demanded

a protective unit for tonight. God, Jussie." He dropped the attitude and looked at her, his gaze filled with concern and other things she didn't want to acknowledge. "Why didn't you tell me you'd had trouble?"

"It happens."

"Not to you, it doesn't," he said forcefully. "Drive safely."

Her anger vanished in the face of the deep worry and stress she read so clearly behind his own temper. "I will."

"Devlin's already there, and he'll call me if there's trouble."

"I'm not an idiot."

"Then prove it," he said, shutting her door. "Go home and *stay*."

She drove off, shaking.

He'd gotten to her. Really gotten to her, and it had to stop. The man was unfairly gorgeous, far too smooth, and . . . oh, hell.

She needed to stop these secret fantasies she had of this becoming a real marriage. It couldn't happen. It was no one's fault. Too much time had gone by.

By the time she'd gotten herself home, Justine had nearly forgotten about the sedan. She'd convinced herself the danger was all in Mitch's head. Who in their right mind would go after the editor in chief of a daily with a circulation of maybe forty thousand? It made no sense.

She had nothing to fear, nothing at all.

Except her feelings for Mitchell Conner.

❧━━━━━━❧

Two hours later she knew she was wrong about having nothing to fear. Devlin had fallen asleep in the living room, his mouth open, softly snoring in tune to the television.

In her office, amid the piles of boxes she'd been using to pack, her fax started humming. Checking the clock, Justine frowned. Who would be using her private fax line at this time of night?

A minute later she had her answer as she studied the message.

BACK OFF OR DIE.

EIGHT

It had taken every ounce of acting ability Justine had to convince a sleep-befuddled Devlin that she needed him to go to Ted and Matt's house for the night. That she needed to be alone.

He'd balked at first, and she'd, well . . . she'd gotten desperate. She'd given him the impression that she was expecting company. *Male* company, in the form of Mitchell Conner. Pride had wanted to deny that, but fear had motivated her. She couldn't leave Devlin in the house alone, not after that threat.

"No big deal," she muttered after Devlin left. "Threats are just a way of life on a newspaper." She'd bet the *Los Angeles Times* had this problem all the time.

Her car flew over the quiet night roads. Strangely enough, she never considered doing anything but driving directly to Mitch's house. The mysterious blue sedan followed her, and for that she was very grateful.

It was hard to miss the biggest, prettiest house in town. But she knew it was all image. Mitch may have spent his early years in high society, but he'd always been on his own, physically *and* emotionally.

Just as she and Devlin had. It had made them kindred spirits back then, during those lean, formative years in high school and beyond.

Frost crunched beneath her feet as she got out of her car and stepped onto the grass. Heels weren't the safest thing to be wearing, but she hadn't taken the time to think about shoes before she'd bolted out the door.

There were lights on inside, thank goodness. She wouldn't have to wake him. A sleepy, ruffled Mitch seemed dangerous, but then again, everything about Mitch seemed dangerous. She knocked on his door, her breath coming out in short, white puffs of air.

She got no answer.

A quick glance behind her assured her the dark sedan had arrived as well, sitting a discreet distance away at the end of the driveway. Watching. Witnessing her humiliation as Mitch avoided this contact with her.

Too much.

Without thinking, she opened the front door, stepped in, and shut it behind her. For one weak moment she leaned back against it. At least now, whatever embarrassing thing happened, she wouldn't have witnesses.

"Mitch?"

Dammit, her voice sounded high and breathless. The folded piece of paper in her pocket reminded her she had reason. "Mitch!"

The house was huge. Her voice echoed strangely. The reason for that was plain—he hadn't gotten any furniture yet. Or very little. The kitchen had two wooden bar stools up against the bar, but no table and chairs. The huge living room with the high-vaulted ceilings was bare, too, with just a high-tech-looking stereo unit and a leather recliner.

Another day, and she might have smiled. To Mitch, music would be far more important than such banal items as a couch. Or even drapes.

Calling his name, she stepped to the bottom of the curved oak staircase and put her hand on it. Despite her fear, curiosity took over. How many times had a young Mitch slid down that tempting banister, face wide with that heart-stopping grin?

It terrified her to discover how much she'd softened toward him. "Mitch?" she called quickly, blocking her thoughts.

He came out of a room on the second floor and stood at the top of the stairs looking down. "Jussie?"

She opened her mouth, but nothing came out.

He had a tiny white towel anchored at his waist. Water dripped freely off his body, from his tousled hair, running in rivulets over his chest. He'd stopped short at the sight of her. Heat flickered in his gaze as it roamed over the clothes she wore—the same he'd nearly torn off her earlier in the storage closet.

He sent her that crooked smile. "You came to tuck me in. How sweet."

Unable to speak for fear her tongue would fall out, she shook her head. God, he was all lean muscle, long limbs, and tanned skin—except for the line of paleness along the top of his towel which barely covered . . . essentials. Water beaded on every inch of his body, making his skin gleam tantalizingly.

He started down the steps, oblivious to the dangerously slipping towel hung so low on his hips. To keep from reaching for the damn thing, Justine clasped her hands tightly. Dazed, she watched him approach her, smelling of soap, wet skin, and *him*.

He shook his head a little, then slicked back his hair. Water flew. "You caught me in the shower."

A drop of moisture ran down the length of his chest, past his flat belly, and disappeared into the towel. Justine swallowed, hard. Then she shivered.

He frowned and took a step closer. "It's freezing outside. Where's your coat?"

"You're . . ." She'd found her tongue, only to trip over it. "Not dressed."

"Nothing you haven't seen before," he said casually, as if she saw nearly nude men—gorgeous and wet, too!— every day of her life. Okay, maybe she *had* seen it all before, but she didn't remember it being so . . . mouthwateringly perfect.

She shivered again.

When he reached for the towel, she panicked, thinking he meant to remove it and wrap it around her. "No!" she cried, lifting a hand. "Don't."

He merely secured it, but gave her a knowing glance. A knowing glance with more than a hint of healthy ego in it. "Okay, so you didn't come to tuck me in." Still smiling, he leaned close. "How about a goodnight kiss?"

"No!" Get a grip, she told herself furiously. *Before he does.* "I—ah . . ." Broad shoulders, firm chest filled her view, made her mouth dry. "Well . . ."

"You look flustered, Jussie." He was amused, his grin a tad wicked.

"Dammit. I came to talk to you. To show you something." Now she sounded prim and annoyed, but it was easier than letting him think she'd been lusting after him.

He laughed. *Laughed*. "Uh-huh. You came to talk." He crossed his arms over his bare, gorgeous chest. "Okay, I'll play, baby. Talk. Go ahead."

"Don't you dare laugh at me," she said, sticking her nose in the air as she struggled for dignity. In the end, she reached into her pocket and slapped the fax against his chest. "I refuse to be a source of amusement to you."

His eyes scanned the short, lethal sentence. Under his healthy bronzed skin, he went pale. "Believe me, little about you amuses me at the moment. When did you get this?"

"Tonight. I think it's because of something that appeared in the *Daily* about the mayor."

He looked at her, his eyes dark and troubled. *"Something?"*

"Controversial items that might have upset him and his supporters. I sent Devlin to a friend's house. I didn't show him the note because he'd just worry." *Goodness, those eyes*. She'd started talking, her words coming faster and faster, as she became unable to stop. "Devlin will be moving there next week anyway, after Christmas, because we have to get out of the house. I'm packing up, so I—"

"Jussie," he said gently, curling an arm around her shoulders. "You're okay now."

No. Definitely not okay. Not when she was wrapped tight against his-still damp side. The heat of his skin blazed through her clothes, but if anything, it made her shiver all the more. "I think . . . it would be best if you got dressed," she whispered.

"You're staying here tonight. Until I put a stop to this."

She'd known he'd say that, had maybe, way deep down, hoped for it. "You don't have a couch."

He feigned ignorance. "Nope. Not yet. I was going to go furniture shopping this weekend."

"Look, Conner—"

"I do have a king-size bed." He grinned, daring her. "Plenty big, I promise."

That voice could coax the light right out of the moon. "A bed the size of this house won't be big enough if *you're* in it."

Now he laughed. "I'll be good." He lifted one hand in the sign of a promise. "Scout's honor."

"That's what I'm afraid of," she muttered, turning her back on the sight of him.

Gently, he turned her around, his hands light on her waist. "You've nothing to fear with me."

Not an ounce of inflection came with that statement, so she had no idea how to take it. But the hunger in his green gaze told her what she needed to know. "I think I'll take the floor. Would you—could you put on some clothes?"

He moved away, depriving her of his body heat. Halfway up the stairs, he let out a little laugh. "Stubborn to the end, Jussie."

It wasn't until he got to the top, and just outside the door of his bedroom, that he dropped his towel.

Mitch couldn't believe it, but Jussie really did prefer the floor over his bed. He cajoled, begged, threatened— nothing could change the woman's mind.

So he settled her on the floor with a pad of thick blankets, then sat on the bed and waited.

It didn't take long. Poor thing had been near exhaustion when she'd arrived. Still, he listened again for her deep, even breathing, then gently scooped her up and put her on his bed, carefully tucking her in. He waited another moment, but she didn't so much as budge.

He'd been flattered before, and more than a little amused at her obvious physical reaction to him, but that had fled in the face of her fear.

He went downstairs to call Hopkins.

His ex-partner answered sleepily, and with more than a little disgruntlement. *"What?"*

"She's been threatened," Mitch said evenly. He knew the value of calm and precision over nerves. Knew that only a cool head could get you through, though none of that meant a damn when it was Jussie being threatened. " 'Back off or die,' the fax said, and I want you to make damn sure it has nothing, absolutely *nothing*, to do with us."

Hopkins swore colorfully. "It couldn't have," he said after a moment. "No way. We made sure you were totally clean before you went back."

"One hundred percent certain."

"Positively. It's got to be something else. Job-related, maybe. Or just a prank."

Mitch stared into space, equally silent. His fault, he thought. But it wasn't fair, when all he'd ever wanted to do was protect her.

"Stop it," Hopkins said quietly.

"I didn't say a word."

"I can hear you anyway. Stop blaming yourself. You

left her for *her* protection, and you went back to her when the threat was gone."

"No, I didn't."

"As soon as you saw the case through, like you promised, you were gone."

"Which took two years longer than expected."

"The point is, you're back with her now, which is where you want to be."

Mitch's stomach suddenly plummeted. "But if there's still something going on, I'll be obligated to leave."

"I never said that."

"You thought it."

"Yes, dammit. We want you back. We've made no secret of that."

"Isn't going to happen."

"This isn't about that," Hopkins promised. "No one is trying to scare you back here."

"How can you be sure?"

"The guy's dead, Mitch. The case is closed, which effectively cut you loose. We've moved on, and there's nothing, not one little thing, left to clear up." He paused. "You're free."

"Good."

"Could it be a gag?"

"It was a damn death threat, Hopkins, not a knock-knock joke. It scared the hell out of her." And me, he thought, shoving his hair back and trying to not think about Jussie's terrified blue eyes when she'd shown him the faxed message.

"Death threats have a nasty habit of being scary," Hopkins agreed. "It's why the bad guys use 'em. I can check it out, have her lines tapped."

"Okay." Mitch rubbed his aching temples. "I'm sorry. This . . . it's been difficult."

"I understand."

He knew Hopkins spoke the truth, that he well understood helpless anger, that he'd felt it firsthand. "Let me know what you find out," he said quietly. "She's getting telephone cranks, too, though she seems to think it's related to her job."

"It probably is. Think about how many articles she puts out daily, how many of those could be considered controversial. This may just be a part of her life that you have to learn to deal with."

"Yeah, well, it blows." Mitch tried to let go of his irritation. He knew Hopkins would do all he could. "Thanks." He hung up and stared into the darkness.

What if they were wrong? What if everything he'd feared about Jussie's safety for the past two years came true? Or worse, what if someone out there hadn't considered his obligation fulfilled? That someone would maybe have access to his records, and his whereabouts.

He knew he shouldn't be doubting his own team, people supposedly on the side of good. But jaded as he was, he'd seen crazier things happen.

His biggest nightmare could still come true, he could see Jussie hurt because of his own actions in hastening back to her.

He climbed the stairs, vowing it wouldn't, then stopped short in the doorway of his bedroom. So did his heart. Moonlight slashed through the room, cutting across the bed. It highlighted her still form, and like a moth to a flame, Mitch moved closer.

She was beautiful. And she was his, dammit. His.

Her hair lay scattered and loose in golds and reds

over his pillow. That face he could never tire of looking at had relaxed in slumber, and he knew if he bent a little more and touched his mouth to hers, it would be soft and giving.

She made a sound, almost a muffled sob, and his gut twisted. Lightly, he ran his fingers down her arm. "Shhh," he whispered. "You're safe here."

Snuggling closer against his pillow, she quieted and sighed. The fist she'd made on the blanket relaxed.

He leaned over her, kissing her on the cheek. Then with a sigh born of sheer self-abnegation, he kicked off his shoes and sat. Leaning back against the headboard, he studied his ceiling and started to plan.

"You moved me," she whispered groggily a minute later.

"Yeah."

"And you think *I'm* stubborn."

The dark cocooned them, enveloped them in a sense of comfort. Ease.

"What are you thinking about?" she asked quietly.

With a wry glance toward the vicinity of the erection threatening the buttons of his Levi's, he said, "Not much."

She snorted and sat up. She swiped at her eyes, pulled the sheet up to her chin, and sat back as well. "You're always thinking about 'not much.' "

Surprise came first, then pleasure. "Was that an admission that maybe you remember more of me than you want to admit?"

"No. And I never said I didn't think of you. I just don't . . . Oh, never mind."

"Come on," he coaxed in the dark. "Finish it."

"I just don't *like* to think of you, all right?"

He let out a short laugh.

She fumbled with the covers for a minute. "Are you sure you're finished with the FBI?"

She *did* think of him, of their future. "I'm not leaving you ever again, Jussie."

"Oh." She went quiet, and there was more fiddling and shifting. A sure sign of her thinking, and thinking hard. "What are you going to do for a living?"

"What I've always wanted. Start my own private-investigating business." Now it was his turn to hesitate. "What do you think?"

She seemed touchingly surprised that he'd asked. "I think you deserve it. You know . . . after all you've been through."

"You went through it too." He turned to her and tried like hell to see her expression in the dark. "I can't possibly be any sorrier than I already am for what happened."

"I know."

"Do you really?"

"Yes." She turned to face him too. "And I don't want you to say it anymore. I won't forget that you've apologized."

"So you've . . . forgiven?"

She let out a breath, drawing his gaze down to the sheet she clutched at her chin. When he'd lifted her to the bed, she'd already been wrapped in blankets. What was she wearing beneath the covers? "Have you?" he asked again, softly. "Forgiven me?"

"Oh, Mitch."

He melted at the sound of his name on her lips, making him realize he didn't hear her say it nearly enough.

"It's not that easy," she answered. "Don't you see?

We've had two years stolen. We'll never get them back. Now you're here, and it's only because they've finally released you from your obligations. Without that, you'd still be gone."

Somehow she believed he'd wanted to stay away. Did she also believe he didn't want her? Amazing as it sounded, it seemed so. "I think we could do with a light now."

"No, I don't want—"

A click of the switch flooded the room with light.

"—the light." Jussie blinked warily and stared at him.

Mitch discovered she wore one of his T-shirts and little else. It thrilled him.

He took one of her hands and brought it to his lips. "I can't deny that I was able to come back because of what happened to the agent. He died, and after the case came to a close, I was free. But I'm here now, where I've wanted to be for so long. Are you going to tell me it doesn't matter? That you don't feel anything for me at all?"

She opened her mouth to speak, but he said quietly, "Careful, Jussie. You're a rotten liar. Besides, I know *exactly* how you responded to me today in that closet. And it wasn't with indifference."

She flushed and tried to pull her hand back, but he lingered over it while his gaze held hers. "Was it?"

"It's not as simple as sex."

"No. Making love isn't simple."

"It wasn't love—"

Her denial was the last straw. "Think again," he snapped back, dropping her hand.

"Well, whatever it was, it was a mistake!" she said,

bringing her hands up to her flaming cheeks. "It was wrong, and we can't do it again."

"You still don't believe me. Dammit, you don't believe a word I've told you."

She blinked and bit her lip, lowering her gaze from his.

"Or that's what you're telling yourself. You tell yourself that I've lied so you don't have to let go of your anger. So you don't have to forgive me. Tell me this, Jussie. Why wouldn't I tell you the truth? Why would I give up my perfect life to run away when I could have had you? And if I was happy being gone, why would I come back? Why? Tell me!"

"I—I don't know." She covered her face.

Restless, angry, and utterly incapable of sitting next to her in a bed without taking her, he leaped to his feet. "It's been a long night. Go to sleep."

"I thought we were talking. . . ." She dropped her hands and stared at him with those huge eyes, her stumbling protest fading. His shirt had slipped off her shoulder, revealing a good bit of a creamy skin that Mitch could already feel under his fingertips.

It didn't improve his mood, nor did the fact that he knew he was wrong to push. "You're not ready to sit and talk with me."

"Meaning?"

Her voice was positively frigid, the kind that would give another man frostbite. But he recognized her defense mechanism well. Just the fact that she was scrambling for control at all made him feel marginally better. "Meaning I have things to say to you, lots of things. But I won't until you're ready to deal with them."

At the bedroom door, he stopped and, for a minute, dropped his forehead to the door.

"Mitch?"

He whipped around, feeling shredded by the ragged hurt inside him. "We're married, dammit. And you're in the spot that I've dreamed about having you for so long."

"This isn't a *real* marriage. If it were, you would never have let them take you without me."

Amazed, he could only look at her. "Is that what you believe? Is that what you really believe?"

She dropped her gaze. "Yes."

"If this was never a marriage, it's only because you never trusted me in the first place."

Throwing back the covers, she stood. Fury flashed. "You're just as impossible as you always were. And just as temperamental!" Bending over, giving him quite a delectable view, she hunted for the shoes she'd kicked off. "I'm *not* staying."

"Oh, yes, you are," he told her backside grimly.

With no regard to her lack of attire, she slipped into her shoes without socks. "Make me."

"Don't tempt me."

"Oh, go ahead!" she demanded, throwing up her hands in disgust. "You're standing there with steam coming out your ears, spoiling for a fight. Let's have it, then. What are you going to do? Lock me in another closet?"

He refused to rise to the bait, though it was tempting. "You're staying until we get to the bottom of this thing with the threats, whether it has to do with the mayor or not."

She glared at him.

"And there's more, Jussie, a lot more, if you wanted to hear it."

She stood on the other side of his bed. The sight of her in his shirt and scanty little panties caused his voice to thicken as if of its own accord. "And if I'm impossible and temperamental, it's because being with you, and not having you, is driving me to the edge. Right to the very edge."

"I won't be bullied into anything," she said, crossing her arms. "Not even by you."

"I know." He felt raw inside, and his throat hurt. "And I'm leaving the room now, because if I don't, I'm going to kiss you. And I won't be able to stop once I get started."

"Whether I want it or not?"

"Oh, you'll want it," he promised, and she swallowed. "I'll do the entire husbandly thing, right there in that bed, and it will take the rest of the night and maybe all of tomorrow, but you'll want it."

As if her knees wouldn't hold her, she sank back to the bed. Her hands, fisted on her thighs, trembled. But she didn't call him back, as he'd hoped she do.

Frustrated, hurt, and horny beyond belief, he sighed. The rage was gone. "Good night, Jussie."

NINE

Dignity came at a high price, Justine discovered the next morning. Fresh out of the shower, wearing only Mitch's white towel, she jerked when the bathroom door opened.

Mitch stuck his head in, caught sight of her, and whistled low, instantly hot and aroused.

"I'm busy," she said through clenched teeth, struggling to keep the wet towel in place.

Slipping the rest of the way into the steamy bathroom, he grinned broadly and offered her a cup of coffee. Despite the heat in his gaze, he lifted a broad shoulder innocently. "I came bearing a peace offering."

She would have been able to hold out, if the brew hadn't smelled so mouthwateringly good. And if his eyes hadn't been filled with such . . . overwhelming things. "Black?" she asked warily.

"Of course."

"Then I accept," she said stiffly, trying not to drool

as she reached for the cup. She'd slept badly, with vague, haunting dreams she couldn't quite remember.

But she'd awakened with tears on her cheeks.

Mitch's gaze swept slowly over her, lingering, heating her cooling, damp skin. She might have found it funny, especially after how she'd felt seeing *him* in the same towel the night before, but there was nothing even remotely amusing about how he looked at her. "Ah . . . Mitch?" When his eyes glazed over and he didn't answer, she made a quick check to make sure she hadn't popped out of the towel. "I think . . . I should get dressed."

"Mmm-hmmm." He ran a finger over the edge of the terry cloth. The tops of her breasts tingled. Her nipples hardened instantly.

"Alone."

His eyes cleared somewhat as he raised his gaze to hers. "You're beautiful."

She felt heat flood her face. For two painful years she'd denied herself male companionship other than the friendship of Jack, and he didn't count since he didn't cause her heart to spiral out of control by just *being*. "Mitch—"

He touched her face, then ran his fingers down her neck, along her bare shoulder. As always when he touched her, her knees started to shake.

"I love the way you say my name," he murmured, watching his fingers on her skin, fingering the gold chain she wore, which disappeared into the towel tucked between her breasts. "I missed that."

"Mitch—"

"Yeah, like that." He exhaled slowly. "I missed everything about you. Everything." He drew her closer, just a little closer, and she could feel herself float toward him, her body moving of its own accord.

"I'm back," he whispered. "And I'm not leaving, not ever again."

"But—"

"Hush." His fingers caressed her lips now, holding in her words. "I want you, Jussie. All of you. I want our lives entwined, the way they were meant to be. But I understand you, probably better than you think. In your life there have been losses, one after another. You've had to fight and work for everything you have. Control is important to you, and right now, in this moment, you have it."

She let out a shaky laugh. "Maybe not as much as you might think."

"You're afraid of this," he said quietly, holding her. "Afraid of me and what I make you feel, and I understand that too. You think if you're not careful, you'll get hurt. Again."

Gently, he cupped her face and tilted it up. Despite her obvious efforts to wash them away, he could see faint traces of tears. It broke his heart. "Isn't that right?"

"I'm not afraid. I just don't want you to play at this husband thing because of some sense of honor."

The feel of her barely covered body, still wet and glistening, was a strain that made his voice rough and grainy. "I think you know I didn't come back for anything other than you. That I've been dying a slow death ever since leaving you." He tilted his head and studied her. Two high spots of color painted her cheeks and she splayed her fingers between their bodies, staring at them.

"Look at me." She did, and he saw her pain and confusion, felt it as his own. "I love you, Jussie. I love you so much."

She gasped, and a gamut of emotions danced across her face, not the least of which were shock and panic. She would have pulled away, but he framed her face, needing to see her. "I never stopped," he told her. "I know you're not ready to hear that, but I can't hide it any longer. I've never loved anyone like I do you. That will *never* change."

"But . . . you don't know me anymore."

"I know you. But I also know you need time. I'm willing to give it, as much at it kills me, because I know you can't be rushed. It took me years to convince you love would be good to you the first time, and I figure it's going to take a while this second time as well." He smiled painfully. "Just be kind while I'm suffering and waiting. Can you do that?"

"You . . . don't know that it can work. Not after all this time."

"No, *you* don't know. But *I* do, and I'm going to show you." His thumbs teased her full lower lip, and her mouth parted on a sigh of wonder at his touch.

This, he thought. This was what he meant to do, always. Show her tenderness and care. Show her that love could be good. That it could heal the heart, cleanse the soul. And since it had been Jussie who'd taught him that lesson long ago, it was fitting he return the favor now.

The steam of her recent shower surrounded them with mist and warmth; the scent of his soap on her skin lent an air of intimacy.

She didn't move as he stepped flush to her. Her hair, the color of sun-touched wheat, dripped over the both of them. Lowering his head, he slid his lips once over hers, gently, patiently. "Let me show you," he whispered softly.

Keep it easy, he told himself hazily, but then she brought her hands up to his arms, tentative at first, then gripping hard, as if she needed the support. Her short, neat nails dug little moons into his biceps as he deepened the kiss. She sighed and pulled closer.

The room buzzed with heat and passion. He still cupped her face, his thumbs sliding over her jaw, her neck. The pulse he found there beat crazily against his fingers, and still, the kiss went on, spinning out time, stealing his breath.

She moaned softly in protest when he lifted his head, but he had to see her face. Her eyes were still closed.

"Jussie."

She opened her eyes, and they were heavy and clouded and so confused, his heart constricted.

"I . . . need to think," she whispered.

He nodded, biting back his disappointment. It couldn't be done in just a few days, he reminded himself. Love was for a lifetime, and for that commitment, he could be patient.

"Definitely need to think," she repeated shakily. She touched her lips, then dropped her hand away, clearly aroused.

He knew the feeling; he was so hard he thought he just might die of it.

"But—" She stared at his mouth, flushing deeply.

"But what?"

"Do you think . . . maybe you could kiss me again first?"

He nearly groaned at her hopeful expression, but held her at arm's length. "Not just this minute, no." If he did, he'd toss her over his shoulder and take her to bed. Forget the bed, he'd take her right here against the counter. "We're going to have to spread those out a little, baby, or your thinking time will be up."

Her cheeks flamed. "I'm sorry. I have no right to ask for that, and not be willing to . . . well, you know."

He laughed, a little painfully. "You can ask anything of me. But I need a minute." And a cold shower.

"It's just that I haven't kissed—no one's made me feel like you—" She bit her lip and covered her face. "Oh, just say something and shut me up, will you?"

"Jussie." Unbearably touched, he reached for her, then stopped himself. Touching her would definitely *not* help. "There's been no one else for me, either," he said, his voice thick with emotion. They'd been each other's first, and there'd not been another woman for him since. "Which is why this is so hard—" He grimaced. "Excuse the unintended pun."

"You mean you haven't—"

"There's been no one else. *Ever*," he repeated softly.

Her eyes warmed, lost a little of her confusion. "I'm glad," she whispered, then laughed nervously. "Not about . . . your, uh, *problem*." Her gaze rested on the vee of his jeans, then widened slightly at the unmistakable bulge she saw there. "But that there's been no one else."

They stared at each other.

"I think . . . I'll get dressed now," she said.

He pushed her gently toward the door. "In the bedroom."

At her bafflement, he slid his hands into his pockets. "I need to shower now."

"You already did."

His smile was wry, crooked, and more than a tad self-mocking. "Yeah, but now I need a *cold* one."

The Christmas spirit had taken hold at the *Daily News*. Wreaths decorated every door and hallway. Goodies and chocolates were laid out in the snack rooms. Festive holiday music filled the air.

Still, there was much to be done. To prove it, Justine threw herself wholeheartedly into work. She moved from one meeting to another, from one problem to another, not stopping for lunch. She couldn't, or she might have time to actually think.

Anne stuck her head around her door. "I can't believe you had enough willpower to skip the lunchroom today. Eddie brought a pound—a *pound*—of candy. The chocolate-covered cherries are to die for."

"Don't tell me."

"Sarah made a three-layer-cake number that's got a minimum of a thousand calories per bite."

Justine smiled grimly. "I'd like to be able to fit into my dress for the Christmas party."

Her secretary studied Justine's petite frame and rolled her eyes. "Uh-huh. Like *that's* going to be a problem." Casually, she glanced into the office next door, where Mitch sat hunched over a computer. "Taking a date this year?"

Justine took the thick stack of files and correspondence from Anne's hands, tossing it next to the drafts she still had to approve. "A date?" She took a quick peek through the window. Mitch had his back to them as he worked, and it occurred to her, she had no idea what it was he was doing in there. They'd agreed this morning he could stick around and prove to himself she was in no immediate danger, but it would be only temporary.

She wondered where he would go when this mess was over, because it was easier to assume he *would* go than to think about what he'd said to her this morning.

In a gut-tightening familiar gesture, he rolled his shoulders. His shirt stretched taut over the muscles in his back, and as she watched he stiffened. Slowly, he looked over his shoulder, and met her gaze straight on, unwavering.

Neither of them smiled, but the look wasn't filled with tension. Instead, it held heat, and promise, and Justine felt her heart rate pick up speed.

She lost track of her conversation with Anne—until the other woman cleared her throat.

Justine jerked her gaze from Mitch's and looked into Anne's amused face. "*What?*"

Anne gave her a knowing glance. "You know what."

Justine sighed. "Are you in here because you don't have enough work? Because—"

"*Are* you bringing a date to the staff Christmas party?"

Justine fiddled with her pencil, then rearranged the papers in front of her. "Why would I do that?"

Anne stuck her tongue in her cheek and bit back a smile. "No reason. No reason at all."

Justine relaxed for a second.

"Except for the incredibly gorgeous man in the next room, who has the other women in this building falling all over themselves in an attempt to get his attention."

Women noticed him? "Don't be ridiculous."

"Forget I asked." Anne inspected her inch-long, green-lacquered fingernails, not making a move to get on with her day.

Justine had to laugh. She put down her pencil. "Okay, let's hear it. You and I both know I'm not going to get any more work done until your curiosity's satisfied."

Unoffended, her friend dug right in. "Well, I figured that since he's your husband, you might want him there. At the party. Especially since he hasn't taken his eyes off you all morning."

"My"—she nearly choked over the word.—"*husband* isn't staff."

"He owns the place, doesn't he?"

That he did. Suitably reminded of the mess she'd allowed herself to get into, she sighed and sat back.

"I'm sorry, Justine. I didn't mean it like that—"

"It's all right, since it's the truth. The sad, sorry truth."

"Well, if it makes you feel any better, just about any one of us would pay to be owned by the likes of him."

Justine looked at her in disbelief. "You're all sick."

"Are you saying you don't think he's magnificent?"

"I . . . hadn't noticed." But she stole another quick glance at the subject of their conversation. The ends of his wavy dark hair curled over his collar, but most of the top stuck up in little tufts from where he'd plowed his hands through it. He was studying his computer screen, scowling, looking rough, dangerous, and so immensely appealing, even her hardened heart lurched.

When she turned back, embarrassed to be caught staring, Anne's eyes were kind. And laughing.

"Oh, geez, invite the poor guy before he gets whiplash from pretending not to watch you while you pretend to not watch him. Besides, can you just imagine how good he'll look in a tux?"

A reluctant smile tugged at Justine's mouth. "Cute buns aren't everything."

"Ah, so you *have* noticed."

Justine studied the notes she'd taken at her meeting with Devlin. His source had hit the jackpot, and now, so had she.

According to her brother, who'd heard it from the as-yet-unnamed source, Mr. Mayor had been busy. He'd accepted huge chunks of money three separate times in the past quarter—all of which could be traced directly back to Q-Vac, the corporation to which he'd declared he had no ties due to their heavy-handed political maneuvering. Not to mention Q-Vac's recent trouble with the Environmental Protection Agency, which had twice fined the corporation for illegal dumping.

Mayor Thompson had high ambitions, all of which would be ruined if proof of these dealings saw the light of day. Justine had asked Devlin, but he didn't know if his source could provide it.

In the meantime several pro-Thompson groups had protested the *Daily News* articles she'd run so far, and she knew she was skating a fine line, especially in such a small town.

The future of the paper was at stake, and she didn't even own the damn thing anymore. But she wanted to; oh, how she wanted it back.

Her world had turned upside down, yet all Justine could think about was Mitch. She'd stopped blaming him for taking advantage of their financial disaster, but as for the other stuff, she didn't know. She just didn't know.

He was back, really back.

The thrill of that caught her unaware at odd times. In the print room, surrounded by twenty-foot machines running paper, where it was so noisy that she couldn't have heard herself speak, she'd conjured up a picture of him. How he'd looked just the night before, wearing only a wicked grin and a clinging towel.

A few minutes later, in the office kitchen, she grabbed some coffee, and remembered how Mitch had looked at her that morning when he'd brought her a cup in his bathroom. His gaze had heated every inch of her skin.

Back in the hallway, she caught a young clerk flirting harmlessly with one of the reporters, laughing and joking. Talking. For a person to whom communication meant everything, Justine realized with a start that for two years she'd talked to no one as she used to talk with Mitch—not Devlin, not Jack, not anyone.

She walked by the conference room, where all the reporters, including her brother, gathered to get their assignments. He looked so young and carefree and happy, it gave her a start. He hadn't looked so open and alive in a long time. Justine knew she had Mitch to thank for that. He'd lavished attention on her brother since he'd been back, whenever he hadn't been trying to lavish it on her.

Everywhere she turned, Mitchell Conner was influencing and changing her life. Yes, for the better, but she still couldn't give in. If she did, she'd lose herself, lose her tightly held control, and she refused to let that happen.

Absolutely refused.

At a time when she should be figuring out her assets, and how to buy back the *Daily News*, when she should be thinking of finding an apartment, since she had only days left in her house, she could think of little but how good it was to have Mitch home.

He drew her out of her shell, stripped away all the layers of protection, until she felt bare and exposed.

Raw.

Justine hated feeling this way, hated the fear it incited, the belly-gnawing, no-holds-barred terror.

She'd felt it far too many times in her life. When her father died and she'd been separated from her brother briefly, before they'd ended up in the same foster home. When she'd had to fight for the right to run the paper her father had left in trust for her. Yes, Justine knew fear firsthand.

But a more recent fear, and a far more devastating one, had come when Mitch had disappeared.

Justine stopped to remind herself that he hadn't left on purpose, but it was hard to remember that, hard to adjust her thinking when she'd believed just the opposite for so long.

But maybe, just maybe, it was time to dwell on the positive.

Mitch hadn't want to leave her, and now he wanted to be married to her. Really married.

And she, a grown woman who had faced many things in her life, was terrified of that.

TEN

Stress drove her to it. Or that's what Justine told herself. She pulled back into the lot of the *Daily News* after a quick lunch break, taking care to make sure she picked a spot at the end of the lot, where the trees hid her car.

She leaned on the outside of her car and sighed with forbidden delight as she took a lick of her triple-decker chocolate ice-cream cone.

Mmm. Nothing like a shot of sugar for tension, she thought, barely containing her moan of pleasure.

She wanted to savor this rare quiet moment to herself before facing an afternoon filled with deadlines, frantic rewrites, and neurotic writers.

Not to mention her *husband*.

She took another lick.

"Jussie, sweetheart, it's forty degrees outside."

The voice was as smooth as her ice cream, but far more unsettling to her system. The body that went with that incredible voice leaned up against her car with a sort of lethal grace.

"Watch the paint job," she said dryly, eyeing her old beat-up Jeep.

Mitch smiled and crossed his long legs. "One of these days, you'll have to bug your husband about buying you a new car."

"I'll buy my own."

His eyes were covered by mirrored sunglasses, but she could have sworn the joy went out of his smile. She felt like she'd kicked a puppy.

Slowly, giving herself time, Justine straightened, adjusted her purse. Shoved her hair away from her face. Then, having run out of things to do, she took another lick.

Mitch watched intently, his glasses tossing back only her own reflection at her. Nervous, she licked again, and this time she couldn't have missed his reaction. He didn't move a muscle, or make a sound, but she felt it just the same.

For an instant, just one weak little instant, she couldn't figure out why she didn't throw herself against that solid chest and let him wrap those wonderful, strong arms around her.

Then she remembered—she no longer knew him, husband or not. And she needed time. "It's a little chilly to be hanging out in the parking lot," she observed, taking another stab at the cone with her tongue.

"It's a little chilly to be eating ice cream," he observed just as evenly, but she detected a roughness in his voice she couldn't identify.

He continued to lean against her car, looking for all the world like he belonged there.

On the highway behind them, cars drove by. In the

distance the drone of a plane added to the din. The sun hid behind a cloud.

And the strangest thing happened. Justine became entirely comfortable standing next to him, saying nothing, doing nothing, but just being. He must have felt the same way, for he tipped his head back and watched the sky, seeming content.

She ate some more and thought about it. Then, because it unnerved her, she stopped thinking altogether. She got to the cone and crunched happily away.

"You used to be a health-food nut," Mitch said casually. "Eating junk food only when you were completely wigged out over something."

Justine swallowed and stared at her cone. This was definitely one of those times she considered herself "wigged out."

"In fact, there've been only three times I ever saw you eat ice cream."

Her gaze jerked to his as memories flooded. "Graduation day," she remembered. "I got my diploma and got sick, I was so nervous."

"That's what happens when you're smart enough to be valedictorian." It gave Mitch a rush of pride, even now, to remember. He'd been several years ahead of her, already in the navy, but he'd gotten leave.

"I gave my speech, then threw up on your shoes." She laughed. "I was mortified."

"For about three minutes," he remembered dryly. "You recovered quickly, and insisted we share a gallon of ice cream. I got all of three bites."

She laughed harder, and it relieved him. Some of the tension had left her shoulders, so he went for the rest. "Do you remember the second time?"

"Yes," she said softly, turning her head away from him to study the oak tree in front of her car.

Gently, he touched her face, turned it back to him. "I'd just proposed to you." He could remember her, standing in the park, where he'd taken her for a picnic. Her hair had been longer then, cascading in rippling golds and reds and ambers down her back. Her huge eyes reflecting their every emotion, with shock and wonder overriding them all. In her shaking fingers had been the diamond ring he'd agonized over.

She didn't wear it now, or the narrow gold band he'd put on her finger at their wedding, and he wondered what she'd done with them. Had she, thinking she'd been deserted, gotten rid of them?

Justine's eyes had closed, and he stroked her cheek once, waiting, wishing.

Her voice sounded dreamy. "You were so . . ." She opened her eyes, and in her first voluntary touch, she covered the hand he had on her face, her fingers brushing over *his* wedding band. "Oh, Mitch. It was so sweet. How you fit the ring into my ice-cream dessert."

"You screamed when you saw it." He grinned, enjoying her mood, her hand on his. "Then you laughed. And cried."

She laughed again, but her eyes were full and wet. "Yeah. You're lucky I didn't throw up on you then too."

It took minimal movement to have their bodies side by side against her car, so that they were thigh to thigh, her head level with his chin. Minimal movement and a whole hell of a lot of feeling. He had only to lean down. Her mouth would be soft and open beneath his. Imagining it nearly drove him crazy, but he wanted *her* to give, so he held back and smiled again.

But because he *was* crazy, and because she was just staring at him, her eyes misty with memories, her forgotten cone dripping down her wrist, he bent forward and licked at the ice cream.

With a little smile, she offered it up, lifting it higher as he took another lick, startling a gasp from her when his tongue took the chocolate from the skin on her wrist instead of the cone. He was close enough, in tune enough, to watch the effect he had on the pulse at the base of her neck. It danced frantically.

"Don't tell me you've forgotten the only other time we shared ice cream together," he murmured huskily as he took another nip from her wrist. "Although technically, it wasn't your choice of dessert, it was mine, so it doesn't count."

She jumped, and would have dropped the cone if he hadn't reached up to steady her arm. Then her jaw dropped. "Oh, my God."

"Yeah." He laughed when she went red again. Shoving the sunglasses up on his head, he looked at her. "You remember, all right."

"I—I can't believe I forgot!"

"Well, it was a pretty hot night," he said. They'd gone out on her patio late one night for a break from the oppressive heat and humidity. They'd started out with a gallon of vanilla ice cream and two spoons.

"You told me I was too uptight."

"You were working so hard, stressing yourself out about your job." He shrugged, grinning. "I was just trying to help you unwind."

"You painted me with ice cream and then . . ."

"And then?" Just the memory of dripping vanilla cream over her quivering skin had him hard as the metal of the car holding him up. A permanent condition these days.

Never a coward, Justine met his gaze straight on, spellbound by the memories. His dark green eyes were bright, fierce. "You ate it off me," she whispered. "Every single bite."

Lost, hot, and aching, that's how he felt. Whatever laughter they'd shared had retreated, dissolved in the face of this nameless, desperate hunger.

"Jussie—"

"I need air," she whispered, shoving the cone at him.

Carefully, he set the cone on the hood of the car and looked at her. "You've got lots of air. We've got a great breeze."

"Then I need room. Move."

Grinning, he did as she asked and moved, *closer*. "How's that?" Before she could smack him, he ducked, laughing. Encircling her waist with his arms, he hauled her up against him. "When are you going to kiss me, Jussie? Kiss me like you used to, with all that sweet fire."

She hesitated.

"Come on, kiss me," he coaxed softly, nudging closer. "I'm that same man, you know. The same one you loved once."

She leaned close, and his heart stopped, thinking she was going to do it.

Then it happened, that sudden instinctive awareness that dissolved the passion and laughter. He froze, trying to place his uneasiness. Training had ingrained a sense of survival, and it kicked into full gear now.

"Mitch." Jussie squirmed free and stepped away. "I—"

"Shh." He stepped closer, his chest brushing against

her back as he surrounded her with his arms. He couldn't have explained it. But he felt it. The hair standing on end at the base of his neck warned him of the evil presence, the danger.

Jussie, obviously, didn't sense a thing. "But—"

"Hush," he said in an almost inaudible voice. As he scanned the area he pushed her gently, firmly, between him and the car, automatically putting her out of range.

Of course, the woman had to fight him. "What—"

"Jussie," he whispered, holding her in place. "Something's wrong."

"What?" She popped her head up over his shoulder, craning her neck.

He had no time to swear at her, though he thought about it. "Down!" he whispered, covering her with his body a split second before the side windows of her car shattered into a million pieces, spraying them with jagged shards.

Before the tinkling of glass had stopped, before Justine could even blink or draw a breath, Mitch grabbed her wrist in an unbreakable grip and tugged.

"Now," he growled in her ear. "Run." When she still hesitated, stunned, he gave her a shove for motivation.

But Justine didn't need motivation, not when another window exploded behind her. Letting out a startled scream, she stumbled.

Mitch pulled her so hard, she thought her arm might pop out of the socket, leaving her little choice but to follow as he raced across the parking lot.

She opened her mouth to protest, to scream, to whimper, but the sound died in her throat when another shot sounded and something whizzed so close to her ear that her hair actually lifted away from her face.

"Faster." Mitch pulled her along with him as he dodged between cars heading toward the Daily News Building, which suddenly seemed miles away. "Faster."

A stitch tore in her side, she lost a shoe, but Mitch ran relentlessly and she kept up.

Then, without warning, he stopped short. She plowed into the back of him hard enough to see stars. Swaying stupidly, she gasped when he ducked and pulled her down beside him, next to a light blue pickup truck. On her knees in the gravel, she panted for air while the man beside her reached down to his ankle and pulled out a gun.

She gasped.

He glanced at her, his concerned gaze running over her, before he turned to peek around the car.

A set of tires peeled, shrieking into the sudden silence.

Justine listened and closed her eyes.

"He got away," Mitch said softly. She heard his gun click, and she could only assume he'd uncocked it, or put the safety on, or did whatever it was one did with a gun.

Slowly she opened her eyes and stared into his. He'd tucked the gun back into its cozy little haven. He ran his hand over her body calmly, but his eyes were anything but calm.

"Are you hurt?" he asked. "Did you get cut?"

"No," she whispered, but he continued to check every inch of her methodically, completely without decorum, even lifting her skirt. Finally satisfied, he hauled her against him to rock slowly.

Heart in her throat, she burrowed in close to the

warmth of him, the broad strength she'd always depended on.

"You're shaking, sweetheart," he whispered, still rocking her.

"No, that's you," she whispered back, wrapping her arms around his neck.

He just held her tighter.

"Mitch?" After a minute she drew a ragged breath. "I need more ice cream."

By the end of the day, Justine felt exhausted, mentally and physically.

The police had come and gone, and a report had been taken. Her shoe had been recovered, minus the heel. Other than the blown-out windows on her car and a couple of bullets big enough to have Justine feeling ill, there was little evidence to go along with the scare of her life.

A kid high on something, the general consensus had been. A coincidence. Justine didn't buy it, and she knew Mitch didn't either. Devlin had turned green when he saw the bullets, but he'd had the local college's football game to cover, and Jussie had made him leave to do his job.

Eventually, as the day ended, Anne left. So did most of the staff. But after an afternoon of answering questions and filling out forms, Justine still had work to do.

Yet she could hardly keep her eyes open.

Delayed shock, she had herself half-convinced, but she was brutally honest, at least when alone, and she knew the shock went far deeper than what had nearly happened in the parking lot.

She could have lost Mitch. *Again.*

She let her head sink to her desk, then she closed her eyes. Just for a second, she thought. Just for a really quick second.

Warm, loving arms. A sweet voice. The only memories she had of her mother.

Then her father, with his kind words and sad eyes.

He, too, was gone.

"Jus!"

The scream, coming from a child's lips, Devlin's, tore at her, ravaged her with grief.

"It's okay, Dev," she told her brother, hugging him tight. "We'll be together again real soon, you'll see," she promised, tears running down her face. "Real soon," she cried as they pried him from her.

Only eleven, she forced herself to watch as Devlin plastered himself to the back window of the car taking him away to his foster home, his face contorted with terror and hurt.

Then, suddenly, she was a young adult, and madly in love for the first time in her life, with Mitchell Conner—loner, favorite bad boy, and fabulous kisser. He graduated and left for the navy. But he always came back, always.

White silk, fragrant flowers, and a heart full of hopes and dreams.

"I love you, Jussie," Mitch whispered. He'd sneaked into the church choir room where she'd been dressing for her walk down the aisle. "I'll always love you." Then a kiss so sweet, so full of love, it'd brought tears to her eyes.

Finally, her forever-after.

But Mitch had disappeared that night, leaving her alone, angry, frightened, and heartbroken.

Now he'd come back.

And, just as quickly, gunshots sounded. She looked down into Mitch's unseeing eyes as blood pumped out of a huge, gaping hole in his chest.

"No!" she screamed, falling deeper into the darkness. "No!"

ELEVEN

From down the hall, where he'd just come back from getting coffee, Mitch heard the soft scream, and his heart leaped in his throat.

Dumping the cup, he charged down the hall, skidding to a halt in the doorway of Justine's office.

She lay over her desk, sobbing quietly.

A quick glance told him they were alone, and after shutting the door, he moved to the desk, dropping to his knees beside her. "Jussie? Baby, what is it?"

A sniffle was all he got, and it broke his heart. He drew in a ragged breath and reassured himself she was okay. That scream, he thought shakily, would haunt his dreams for a long time to come.

She was quietly crying as if she'd never stop; deep, gut-wrenching sobs that brought a lump to his own throat. He took her in his arms as if it were the most natural thing in the world—and it was.

All he knew was that she hurt, and he'd do anything

to fix it. Rising, he sat in the chair he'd just pulled her out of.

Suddenly she jerked and gasped, and instinctively his arms tightened as his eyes scanned the room, his body tense with the need to protect. Then he realized that she'd been sleeping, but he knew by her absolute still-ness that she was awake. Cradling her head against his shoulder, he stroked her hair. The love that welled within him felt like a two-fisted punch, but it didn't sur-prise him. Everything about Jussie was bittersweet. He loved her, he'd *always* loved her, and he couldn't see how this could be wrong.

"Jussie," he whispered. "You were dreaming."

"Did—did anyone see? Hear me?"

How she'd hate that, having someone, even him, see her out of control. "No, we're alone," he assured her, and when she still didn't relax, he sighed. Slipping out from beneath her, he left the room, crossed into his of-fice where the blinds were, and closed them. Then he came back, shutting and locking the door.

"No one but us," he said.

She nodded shakily and swiped roughly at her tears, avoiding his gaze. "I'll just go—"

"Nowhere." Crossing back to her desk, he easily lifted her back against him and sat down with her on his lap. "You'll go nowhere. You're still shaking like crazy." He hugged her close. "Hold on to me."

She closed her eyes instead.

In a gesture he hoped was soothing, he stroked her hair again, keeping her snug against him. "Was it about the shooting?"

She shook her head.

"Tell me."

He watched her fight against the tears. It hurt him to see her silent struggle to block him out. For so long he'd been on his own. He'd thought he'd never be with anyone ever again. He'd had no one but himself, let nothing touch his heart . . . until he'd come back. Until Jussie, who'd jump-started his emotions, who was his life, even if she'd done her best to hold back from him.

No more, he promised. There'd be no more holding back—for either one of them. He gathered her as close as possible, though she resisted each movement, holding herself stiff as a board. "I'm here now," he whispered. "And I'm not going anywhere, I promise. Let it out, Jussie, let it all out, for once."

Still, she held herself rigid, and he even imagined she was holding her breath. Bending, he gently brushed his face to hers, letting their cheeks touch. Then he kissed her temple. "Come on, sweetheart, it's okay. You've got to at least breathe."

It started with a shudder, then a low moan. The tears came then, in a gushing flow, soaking his shirt. He pulled her closer, and she grabbed fistfuls of his shirt and held on tight. He let her cry, murmuring meaningless words, running his hands over her slender shoulders and back, feeling protective and helpless and strong and weak all at the same time.

It took a long time, but the fierceness of her embrace lessened somewhat, and so did her sobs. And after a storm like that, he had to wonder . . . had she not let go in the entire time he'd been gone?

Knowing her, probably not. It made him suddenly feel like crying himself.

He could have lost her today, just like that.

"It was just a dream," she said eventually, in a rusty voice. "I'm sorry."

"Don't be."

"I was remembering . . ." She sighed. "It sounds so pathetic now, but I was remembering all the times I'd lost someone. Or needed someone and they weren't there."

"You'll never lose me again, Jussie."

"I could have this afternoon."

"No. I'm trained for exactly this, you know that. I'm going to keep both of us safe, I promise you."

She pressed her face into his chest. Her small, very sexy body burrowed into his, which reacted with such a sharp jolt of desire, it stole his breath.

She needed him, he reminded himself as his hands started to roam, as his nerve endings reacted to the heat and the electric current running between them. She needed him, just to *be*, not to be wondering how soft that couch against the wall of her office would feel beneath her writhing body. He bit back his moan, barely.

"I'm fine," she whispered, but she didn't let go. "I can get up now."

Let her up before you do something stupid and rash that you'll both regret. But he didn't let go. He couldn't.

She murmured his name. Afraid it was a protest, he kissed her cheek softly. "Let me touch you, Jussie. I need . . . you. *This*." Brushing his lips over her damp cheek, then her temple, he inhaled her scent. The hunger he felt surged within him, and despite his long abstinence, it was only partially physical. He wanted *her*, the woman beneath the exterior, and he'd become desperate for a glimpse.

When his lips swept the tempting corner of her

mouth, she made a small sound in the back of her throat. Maybe another man could have resisted, but not him. Starved for her affection, trembling with the force of his emotions, Mitch sighed in relief when she wound her arms around his neck. She whispered his name as she pressed even closer, and he found himself uncertain who was comforting whom, but it no longer mattered.

Need took over.

He started with a whisper of a kiss, the lightest of brushes of mouth against mouth. Then he kissed her again, putting his whole heart into that one short, sweet connection.

Carefully, he retreated, to find her eyes blinking in surprise and confusion as she watched him.

"I'm going to kiss you again," he said softly.

"Mitch—"

"And again."

Her lips parted, her expression swirled with things he was afraid to think about. Desire grew as he came back and toyed with her giving mouth some more, until he heard a whimper escape her throat.

"God, Jussie. I want you." He punctuated each word with a meeting of their lips as he roamed her beloved face. "I want you so much."

Her mouth opened, and he kissed her again, moving slowly, sensuously. Somewhere along the way he'd gentled his own raging needs, and he hesitated, wanting her, yet fearing she'd turn him away. "Please," he whispered, waiting for some sign, for a voluntary move that showed him she welcomed this.

Slowly she pulled back and stared at him. Just as slowly she reached up, sank her fingers into his hair, then she was pulling, drawing him back to her.

With her encased in his arms, he rose to his feet in one fluid motion, so that she gripped him tight with a soft gasp. Slowly, he lowered her to the couch, layering his body over hers.

Leather creaked pleasantly beneath them, giving with the new weight. Holding her head with one hand, his other touched her face, his fingertips skimming over the features he'd dreamed about for so long.

"It's the same," she said, her eyes closed, her head falling back against his arm. "I'd wondered, you know. I used to feel like I was on fire from the inside out when you touched me. I still feel it."

Passion leaped within him, as hot as the fire she spoke about. His fingers threaded through the silk of her hair. *More.* It was all he could think, even as her scent, her taste swam in his head. He touched her then, finding the curves and planes of her body by memory. Nothing had ever felt so good.

More.

He tugged open her blouse, desperate to feel, to taste, to touch what he already knew would be perfection. Snapping off buttons in his hurry, he dragged his mouth over her now-bared shoulder, racing over smooth, delicious skin, and stopped short. He jerked a stunned, disbelieving gaze to hers.

Eyes shining brightly, she lifted the gold chain she wore. Her diamond ring and narrow gold wedding band dangled at the end of it. "I kept them," she whispered. "In case you were wondering."

"I was." He swallowed, hard. "You kept them close to your heart."

"I figured it was where they belonged."

"Oh, Jussie." Lowering his lips, he kissed the precise

spot between her breasts where the rings had rested. "Someday, you're going to let me put those back on your finger."

"Mitch." She could only say his name, any more than that eluded her. The hot, desperate need took her by surprise, but the surge of emotion didn't. She'd known how it would consume, she'd known it would be impossible to turn away from, but even so, she couldn't regret it. All she could do was shove the fear and weakness back to another place, and hang on.

She wasn't alone in this. The pain and longing in Mitch's deep green gaze told her that. He pulled her closer, sliding a slightly trembling hand down her spine as he pushed the blouse from her. He wasn't afraid to show how he felt. Freely, he let her see *his* weakness, *his* need, *his* arousal. She closed her eyes and let him bring her closer and closer to the heat.

"This won't change anything," she managed to say on her last coherent thought. He dipped his head to kiss her breast through her bra. She gasped at the unexpected bolt of fire. "It . . ." She lost track of her words when he slipped the lace barrier from her, skimming fingertips over the tight and aching peaks. "It . . . won't."

"Shhh." His voice was thick, husky. "God, you're so beautiful. Don't think, Jussie. Not now. Just feel."

She could do little else when he reared up and pulled his shirt off, flinging it aside. The small light on her desk played over the ridges and planes of muscle in his chest, his shoulders. It was a body born of pure physical labor, not the calculated build from a gym and weights. She stared, unable to help herself, while his flat belly rose and fell softly with his accelerated breathing.

"You're beautiful too," she whispered, touching him. Beneath her fingers his muscles leaped. *Because she'd touched him.* For a minute it brought her out of the magical mist of desire, and she hesitated. "Mitch . . . this is just a physical reaction." She'd meant it as a statement, but it came out more as a question. "Just a meeting of our bodies."

Curling a hand around hers, he brought it first to his lips, then lower, and she thought he meant to bring it to his erection.

Instead, in a heartrending gesture, he pressed her hand to his chest. Beneath their entwined fingers she could feel the solid beat of his heart. "Make no mistake about it, Jussie," he whispered, his eyes dark, fathomless. "It's a meeting of our souls."

When she might have spoken again, he kissed her, hotter, hungrier, and she gave herself up to it. Impatient for the feel of his skin against hers, she urged him down, closer, until they rested side by side, heart to heart.

"Shouldn't we turn off the light—" Her words were cut off by his mouth, by the things his hands were doing to her. Before she could draw another breath, he'd taken care of the rest of her clothing.

"I want to see you, watch you," he said hoarsely, watching his fingers on her as they trailed over taut, quivering thighs. "I want to know this is real and not just another fantasy."

"You've—" Her breath caught when his rough, clever hands rushed over her flesh. "You've fantasized about me?"

"Oh, yeah," he whispered, dipping his head to taste greedily. She bucked off the couch and into his arms when he sucked a pebbled nipple into his mouth, teasing the tip with his tongue. His hard thigh slipped between her softer ones, riding high, higher, until he touched the heat of her. "I've dreamed about this every godforsaken night of the past two years," he rasped, moving his leg until she moaned.

Shattering, soul-destroying wonder. It filled her, leaving no room for shyness in the lit room, and certainly no room for awkwardness. She had been sure there would be, since it'd been so long. But she should have known this, with him, would be as magical as she'd remembered.

Unhurried, Mitch took his hands, his lips and tongue, on a journey down memory lane. He'd lost himself, utterly and irrevocably. Each quick little shiver he coaxed, each little sound she made, brought him closer to the edge, until he thought he might go mad.

More. He continued to nibble her while his hand slid up her thighs, and oh God, found her wet and burning. A soft, strangled breath caught in Jussie's throat, and she clutched at his shoulders, gripping hard. Another touch, and she started to shake violently, and he knew she was on the verge of letting go, but fighting it every step of the way, terrified and exhilarated all at once.

"Don't hold back," he said in a determined and very shaky voice. "Not ever again." Dizzy and desperate, he kissed her slow and deep.

This time when he stroked her, teasing and tormenting, her body bowed in pleasure and shock. Relentless, his fingers moved, playing over her until she panted for breath.

"Wait." She gasped. "Wait."

He didn't let up, and with one more soft touch, she sobbed out his name, convulsing as she came into his hand. Unbearably aroused, he lifted his head to watch her as she shattered, holding her wide, blue gaze until she closed her eyes.

"Look at me. God, Jussie, look, and know what you do to me."

Justine's eyes flew open, hazy and shadowed as she tried to focus after being stripped of any semblance of control. Mitch smiled a wobbly smile, and kissed her. Dazed, she slipped her arms down his back, and found it damp with strain and passion. She could feel his arms trembling as he held himself over her, and power and wonder surged through her. That she could make this strong man weak with wanting awed her. She traced her fingertips down his spine, then slowly around, and found him.

He sucked his breath in through his teeth. Encouraged, she encircled him and stroked, and a shudder rippled through his entire body.

He drew away from her long enough to reach over her to the floor and into his pants for his wallet, and the foil packet he kept there.

"I'm safe," he said quietly into her questioning eyes. "But I don't want to add to your list of grievances against me, not now, not when I'm hoping I'm getting closer to your heart."

To her heart *and* soul, she thought as he braced himself over her. She arched up to meet him, but as he pressed against her, she tightened in nervous anticipation.

Mitch kissed her again until her muscles gave a bit, but his own control had obviously slipped badly.

He groaned, shaking with the effort to hold back. He slid his hands beneath her hips, along the back of her thighs, drawing her legs up. "That's it, sweetheart," he murmured. "Relax, baby. Yeah, like that." He lifted her onto him until he could sink slowly into her, deeper and deeper, until he was halfway to a climax and hadn't even moved within her.

Then, he found a rhythm as natural as breathing. He watched her eyes glaze over, heard her let go with an erotic sigh of pleasure as he slid in and out of her body. Her hands rushed over him, soothing, urging, frantic, and he bent to taste her again.

Their gazes met, and Mitch would have sworn he could see her soul, and his, mirrored there. Stripped completely bare.

He understood her fear suddenly, but understood as well, that they were in this together, that wherever they ended up, they'd at least be with each other.

Jussie cried out, and shattered around him, and he was right behind her, lost in her arms as a climax came in waves and waves, relentless, powerful—an explosion of fierce, pure love.

Justine stared at the light flickering on her desk and listened to the rhythm of Mitch's breathing as it returned to normal. It was unbelievably soothing, as was the not-so-steady drum of his heart.

She felt his lips on her shoulder, and smiled. She hugged him close, and he lifted his head and kissed her.

"Was that the same as you remembered?" she asked, sliding her fingertips lightly down his spine until he shivered.

His smile split into a grin as he levered himself up on

his elbows to ease his weight from her. "Are you asking if it was good for me?"

"I—well . . ." She trailed off, embarrassed, even more so when he laughed softly, tipped to his side, and brought her with him.

He bent close and covered her mouth with his in a quick, tender, possessive kiss. "It's always good between us, no matter what we're doing. This is just one of those ways it happens to be fantastic."

She shivered then, a remnant of either great sex or regret, she had no idea which. Mitch ran a finger over the goose bumps on her arms, then got up to search for their haphazardly tossed clothes.

She got up as well, and standing there naked, she glanced over at her fax.

She let out a choked cry, suddenly trembling from head to toe.

"Jussie?"

Slowly she held up a sheet that must have come in between the time she'd fallen asleep at her desk and when Mitch had come in to wake her from her nightmare.

LAST WARNING—BACK OFF OR DIE.

Mitch had promised himself he'd give Jussie the distance she seemed to need, but he had no intention of letting her out of his sight ever again.

And when it was all done and over, he'd probably be eligible for sainthood, but he had to do it.

He took her to his house, the car ride silent and tense. Once there, he'd gently pushed a still-shaking Jussie into his bathroom, telling her to take a hot shower, hoping it would dispel the shock.

And give him time to get himself under control.

But when he found her standing alone and forlorn in front of the sink, dripping wet, eyes wide and frightened, he caved in instantly. "Oh, sweetheart," he murmured, gathering her close. "I'm sorry, so sorry."

"Hold me."

Since he already was, he just hugged her tighter. Then he carried her into his bedroom to tuck her into his huge bed.

Did she want to be alone? Too bad, he couldn't be that understanding.

He leaned over her. Just one kiss, he promised himself. Just one.

But she tipped her head up and clung unexpectedly.

"Jussie," he whispered as they rolled over and over, tangling hopelessly in the sheets. "I love you—"

She kissed him fiercely, cutting off his words. "Just don't leave me alone," she whispered back, running her hands over him. "Not tonight."

Not ever, he promised silently, and let her take him.

TWELVE

Mitch took some comfort during the day in the knowledge that he could at least see Jussie, and be sure she was safe. He liked the glass between their offices, and liked even more how many times he caught her staring at him.

But even after making love until dawn, he knew that she still needed time, that she still didn't fully trust him with her heart.

Forcing his mind and eyes off her, he turned to the computer at his disposal. Computers had always been a special talent of his, and he planned on making the most of that talent now.

He'd tried getting Hopkins yesterday, several times, but for the first time in their relationship the agent had been unavailable.

In a matter of minutes Mitch made a stranger discovery. His access codes, the ones he'd used for two years, came back denied. He tried again, and then again, with the same result.

He felt no panic. His training was too deeply ingrained for that. Following instincts had become second nature in the navy, then later in the FBI, and he used those instincts now. Against rules, he risked a call to Hopkins on the newspaper phone, using the familiar long series of numbers he'd been given years ago.

He was disconnected three times in a row, leaving no doubt.

He'd been cut off.

Without a thought to the FBI's sensibilities, he calmly and efficiently hacked his way into their computer files. Technically he was breaking the law, but he knew he'd do much worse to keep Jussie and Devlin safe.

Much worse.

But he found it didn't matter. Not when his case, and any evidence of it, had been wiped from the system.

Mitchell Conner, at least in the eyes of the government, no longer existed.

Jussie decided the heck with fitting into her Christmas dress and popped a third cream-filled chocolate into her mouth.

"That's disgusting. You can eat that crap and still sport that to-die-for body."

Justine groaned and turned to face Mitzy. If anyone's body was perfect, it was Mitzy's. She wore a skintight banana-yellow shirtdress and her jet-black hair had been carefully designed in a rave retro seventies look. Despite Justine's dislike of the meddling woman, she had to admit—Mitzy looked striking. "This is a company kitchen," she pointed out coolly. "In other words, for staff that hasn't been suspended."

Mitzy smiled, unperturbed. "Darn. I thought you'd be happy to see me."

"Not quite."

"So . . ." She wandered into the room. "Haven't forgiven me yet, huh?"

Justine would *not* let this woman get under her skin. She wouldn't. "Don't you have a party to go to? Some tea or maybe a luncheon to attend? Some charity event to rip off?"

Uninsulted, Mitzy laughed. "Sounds like fun, huh?" She preened and smoothed a nonexistent wrinkle. "Maybe you're jealous."

"Don't be ridiculous."

"No?" Mitzy looked up, for once her eyes clear of mockery. "Then why don't you like me?"

The surprisingly sincere question stopped Justine cold. And since she'd never in her life purposely hurt anyone, she answered carefully, "I don't know you enough to not like you."

"Hmm." Mitzy eyes glittered once again.

"What is it you want?" Justine asked wearily. She glanced at the chocolates, nearly tempted to swallow another.

"My job. Give me another chance. Drop the suspension."

"No." Temptation gave way to weakness, and she went for another chocolate. It was heavenly.

"Better *back off* the candy," Mitzy said in a soft voice, nodding to the tray of candy. "*Or die* . . . of high cholesterol."

Justine froze, stunned. The blood roared in her head, her vision clouded. *Back off or die*, her messages had said. Twice.

My God, she thought, then whipped her head up to face Mitzy.

She was gone.

When Mitch picked up his phone and heard Hopkins's voice, he sagged with a rush of relief. "Where the hell have you been?"

"Hello to you too." Hopkins laughed. "And I always thought this was so one-sided."

When Mitch didn't respond with the obvious quip, Hopkins sobered immediately. "What's the matter?"

"Oh, I don't know," Mitch said sarcastically. "Maybe it's because I'm no longer on your system. Or that I got ejected when I used my access code, the one that you assured me would be there for the rest of my life. Then I can't get you by phone. I thought we were closer than this, Hop—"

"Hey," Hopkins said quickly. "Wait a minute. *Wait a minute.* There happens to have been a hell of a communications failure here yesterday, and my phone was out. Now I know that just ruffles your panties, big guy, but it's not my fault."

"What happened to the computer?"

"It's complicated. But it's handled now. If it inconvenienced you, I'm sorry, but—"

"*Inconvenienced.*" Mitch laughed harshly. "That's a good one, Hop. No, I wasn't inconvenienced, not much, except for the new gray hairs I'm sporting. I thought I'm supposed to be able to get you, *always.*"

"Mitch," Hopkins said gently. "Flattered as I am that you call me at all, you're not in the program any longer."

Mitch did a double take, then laughed shakily. "God, you're right." He ran a hand over his face. "For two years you were my only contact, and I—well, hell."

"It's all right." A huge sigh came over the line. "I should have prepared you better, but there wasn't time. Most guys have this problem at first. It's natural. I was your only steady contact for so long. As for the computer access, your security level has been switched. After you called last, and we talked about Jussie's threats, I upgraded you again, just in case. I'll get you the new codes ASAP, but I felt it important to ensure no one could get to you."

"Not even me." So logical. God, he felt stupid. "Okay. Thanks. I guess I thought I'd been ditched."

"*Are you kidding?* After how hard I worked to get you in the first place? And as for the other thing, let's get this clear." He lowered his voice and spoke urgently. "You know, dammit, *you know* you're as close to me as anyone."

Mitch had thought so. He knew Hopkins didn't like many people, was grumpy as hell to most, and had let no one other than Mitch into his life, especially after Carol's death.

"Are we straight?"

It was as close to a confession about their strong friendship as Mitch was going to get. "Yes," he said, which was as close as Hopkins was going to get to the same thing. "Someone took potshots at us in the parking lot yesterday. Justine thinks it has to do with the mayor and some articles about him in the paper. What can you give me?"

"I'll check him out, first thing. Consider us on it,

Mitch, but it might be slow. Half my staff just got pulled for another case."

"Another case isn't my problem," Mitch said quietly, calmly. "And I know you owe me nothing, but everything I care about is on the line here."

"I know. But all you have is a threat at this point. I've got another case where three agents were killed, and their families are demanding answers. I'll get back to you soon as I can. Okay?"

What else could he say? "Yeah." Frustrated, he set the phone down and shoved all ten fingers through his hair.

There was no reason for this little niggling of doubt he couldn't get rid of. No reason at all.

He'd do what he had to do to protect Jussie.

To start with, he had certain items to take care of. While working for the government, he'd always been provided with housing. Thanks to that, he'd put away nearly every penny he'd ever made. Boredom during the past two years had led to investing, and he'd turned out to be surprisingly good at it.

The proceeds had allowed him to finance his childhood home, the *Daily News*, and now one last major purchase.

Despite Jussie's certain fury, he placed a bid on her house. The offer he gave the bank was high enough that he had no doubt he'd be awarded the property. What he *did* doubt, however, was how Jussie would take to her Christmas present.

Next, he set about the chore of tracing Jussie's threatening faxes. If he didn't, if he stopped to think, he might remember how it felt to know he'd almost lost her.

How it felt to be in the middle of that parking lot knowing he might not be able to keep a bullet from tearing into her precious skin.

God. It was at times like these that he missed the physical training of the navy. He could use an outlet for this simmering violence.

It was then he happened to glance up.

In the next office, where his wife was bent over what looked like stacks of work, Jack walked in.

No harm in that, Mitch said to himself when his entire body went tense. No harm at all. After all, she and Jack worked together, and Jack probably came into her office on a daily basis.

But then Jack smiled.

And Jussie smiled back; a wide, open, carefree smile such as he hadn't seen since . . . *Dammit*. Mitch had never seen one like that, not since he'd returned.

Early this morning, she'd gone back to her house and covered that sweet, delectable body in a tailored shirt-dress the color of her eyes. Now she looked good enough to eat. But she seemed oblivious to that, and to the fact that when she leaned close to take the files Jack handed her, her bodice gaped slightly, revealing the pale, perfect slope of a breast.

The pencil in Mitch's hands snapped in two.

In the next office, she laughed. Then she leaned a hip back against her desk and swung a long, lovely leg.

Mitch grated his teeth and growled when Jack took a good, long look at those legs as Jussie stretched and reached for her ringing phone.

His wife.

Those were *his* legs to look at, Mitch decided—not Jack's.

Jussie laughed again at something Jack, the soon-to-be-dead man, said. Smiling, Jack took her hand and pressed it to his own chest in a romantic gesture that had steam coming from Mitch's ears. That was *his* move!

Now he was going to have to kill them both, Mitch decided, rising slowly. Halfway to the door, he stopped short.

The green monster had gotten the best of him.

He might have laughed, but since he couldn't seem to find the humor, he kept going.

He needed a fight.

Justine looked up as Mitch stormed in, and she let out an involuntary gasp of . . . awareness.

Never one to give much thought to his attire, Mitch typically wore jeans. Now was no exception, she noticed, and although faded, they were clean, and emphasized his toned, sexy body. He wore a blue cotton button-down shirt, which, in an effort to adhere to the dress code, he'd even tucked in. But the sleeves had long ago been shoved up, the collar loosened.

Yet it wasn't his clothes, or even the body in them, that drew her now. Nope. It was his dark expression—earthy, a little wild, and more than a little dangerous.

"Mitch." Jack, undeterred, leaned back and nodded curtly.

"Jack." But Mitch didn't even glance at him. He came straight for her, and before he'd taken three steps, Justine's heart threatened to burst from her chest.

She tried to ignore him, an impossible feat as the full six feet of raging sexuality loomed closer. "We're working on . . ." Oh, dear. What had they been working on? Helplessly, she glanced at Jack.

Jack, obviously amused at the way her mind had emptied like a leaky bucket, only raised an eyebrow. Damn them both, she thought. "Well, we're busy," she finished lamely.

Given the way Mitch took a chair directly between her and Jack, her words had fallen on deaf ears. Apparently, Mitchell Conner planned on staying. Well, she couldn't possibly work with him sitting there. Good God, she could hardly think.

He smiled at her, though it didn't come close to reaching his eyes. She took a second, deeper look at him, suddenly concerned. Beneath that explosive exterior was an utter despair she didn't understand. "Mitch?"

"I'll just wait," he said in a voice of unbendable steel. He blinked and the flash of vulnerability disappeared, leaving her wondering if she'd been seeing things.

Mitchell Conner was not vulnerable.

"It's not necessary to wait for me," she said. "We might be a while."

Jack and Mitch were staring at each other, having that male conversation without words again. The one women needed a decoder ring to understand.

Neither looked pleased.

Justine sighed. "Oh, for goodness' sake." She scooped up her proofs and headed for the door. "I'll be in copy editing, when the two of you are done. The testosterone level is getting way too high in here for me."

She didn't hear a peep as she shut the door.

Because neither of them spoke for a long moment.

"Well," Jack said, staring at Mitch.

"Well." Mitch met his steady gaze.

"You're back." Jack nodded toward Justine's desk. "Got her shaken up but good too. Was that your plan?"

"I'm sure this is none of your business," Mitch said evenly, knowing Jack referred to Mitch's reappearance, not what had happened to them in the parking lot yesterday. The entire staff seemed to take the incident in stride, assuming it'd been a senseless drive-by shooting that even small towns such as Heather Bay suffered.

"What concerns Justine concerns me," Jack said just as evenly.

That Jack wasn't cowed by the fact Mitch signed his paychecks brought the man up marginally in Mitch's esteem. *Marginally.* "She's my wife. And your editor in chief."

"And one of my closest friends."

"Friends?" Mitch relaxed at these words only because Justine had made it clear there'd been no one else for her, and he trusted her implicitly. It was Jack he didn't trust.

"Friends," Jack said firmly. "The best of."

It was wrong to be jealous of that. He should be grateful she'd had someone so obviously strong in character, so protective.

But a small part of him still resented it.

Jack looked in him in the eye. "Do you have any idea what happened to her when you left? The things people whispered behind her back?"

He told himself that smashing Jack's pretty face wouldn't make him feel better, but he still had to force his fists to flatten against his thighs. "No."

"Do you know how hard it was for her not only to continue working here, but to work her way up through the ranks to get where she is, especially when people wondered if she could handle it?" Jack eyed him critically. "She's the strongest woman I know, but her pride has taken more than its fair share of beatings."

Killing Jack wasn't going to be enough, Mitch decided. He was going to have to kill Hopkins, too, for making Jussie suffer needlessly.

He felt physically sick over the image Jack painted of her struggling on her own. She'd faced so many battles in her life, and the amazing, resilient woman had come through them all.

She'd grown and matured since he'd been with her, tremendously. She had huge responsibilities, and great demands on her time. But he had to believe there was still room for their relationship in her life.

"I realize I'm probably out of line here," Jack admitted stiffly. "But I won't see her hurt again."

Mitch decided love was far more important than pride. "I didn't leave her on purpose," he said gruffly.

"I think you should stay the hell away from her."

"I didn't ask what you think." He stood. "I've come back for my *wife*, Jack."

Jack just glared at him.

Defensive as it was, Mitch felt the need to justify his behavior. "And I don't ever plan on leaving. I'm going to do whatever it takes to make her believe that, even if I have to dog her side every day for the rest of my life. If you have a problem with that, too damn bad."

Jack studied him seriously for a long moment, before letting out a small, encouraging smile. "Nope. No problem. *Boss*." He stood as well. "But there's something you should know."

"Yeah? What's that?"

"If you screw up again, I most definitely won't." Jack moved to the door, where he hesitated. "Want a hint?"

"Will you promise to go away?"

"Yeah. Try kissing up."

Mitch stared at him.

"You were in the navy," Jack said with a broad grin. "I know you know what I mean."

"Why don't you spell it out for me?" Mitch suggested unpleasantly.

"Nothing pleases a woman like being fawned over. Seems to me Justine hasn't been fawned over nearly enough."

Mitch watched the door shut behind Jack and had to let out a little laugh. Damn if the man wasn't right.

He'd come back wanting Jussie back so badly, he'd forgotten the essentials of what he'd learned about women.

He'd tried bullying, cajoling, breaking the law . . . even begging.

But he'd never once tried wooing.

THIRTEEN

Though it was true that a newspaper staff never slept, most of them had left for the night when Justine got yet another hang-up call.

It unnerved her more than she wanted to admit, and for a moment she just looked at the phone as if she expected it to reach up suddenly and bite her. She was so intent on this, she missed Mitch's reaction in the other room, missed his sharp oath and the way he watched her carefully before leaving his office.

"You can forget about going home alone tonight," he said, entering her office.

She took a deep breath before turning to face his deep, concerned voice. "I don't think so, but I do need to talk to you before I go."

Mitch's eyes darkened. His jaw clenched. But his voice remained neutral. "Don't fight me on this."

That voice. It reminded her of feathery touches, dangerous kisses, and a hot passion she'd do well to put out of her mind. "I can't stay with you again tonight. I need to think, and it's not fair to you to—"

"Don't." He put a fingertip to her lips, then dropped his forehead to hers. "God, Jussie. Do you think I'm going to push you to do something you don't want? Or are you afraid you'll forget you don't want it? I just want you safe, dammit."

Suddenly she knew. He blamed himself. Emotion clogged her throat and she reached out to touch his arm, finding it corded with tension. "It's not your fault, Mitch," she said. "What's happening is not your fault."

"You don't know that." He backed away from her touch, his big hands plowing through his hair. The movement drew Justine's eye to his arms, his muscles stretched taut.

"Those shots weren't random," he said roughly. "And these crank calls and threats . . . you looking so tired, you could keel over at any second."

"Mitch—"

"And you getting hurt when I left—"

"Mitch, stop it." She let out an involuntary sound of sorrow. "I don't think I'm in any real danger."

"Why?"

"I think it's Mitzy trying to scare me for suspending her."

"Mitzy?"

"I don't know the why of it yet, but I will," she said, reaching for his hand. "The point is, you're not at fault here. And . . . as for what happened two years ago, you never meant to hurt me."

"No." His voice lowered. "But you still don't want to hop back into a marriage with me."

Her lips curved at his look of self-disgust. "I never said I wanted out either."

His big body went still. "No, you haven't. Jussie, is it too soon to ask what you *do* want?"

"Yes," she said softly. "It is."

"You feel nothing, then."

"No!" she denied quickly, then smiled a little when she saw sudden triumph and hope in his gaze. "You know damn well we seem to . . . set each other off."

He blinked innocently. "Set each other off?"

"You know. We . . . we're . . ." Dammit. He could so easily fluster her. "We're a bit attracted to each other."

He laughed and shook his head. "Oh, Jussie. Isn't that just the understatement of the year." He toyed with her hair, stroked her jaw, and ran his fingers down her spine until she leaned into him. "Just a *little* attracted, huh?" His eyes flamed and he dipped his head, skimming his lips with a featherlight touch over her face until she actually moaned softly.

He lifted his head and pierced her with a knowing stare. "We set each other on fire, baby, and you know it."

"I'm trying to talk to you," she said weakly.

"So talk." His lips continued to cruise, causing a shiver. But he lifted his head when she kept herself still.

"I don't want to toy with your feelings," she said softly, close to begging for more. "I would never do that to you, but this is difficult for me. I'm just not ready to . . . set each other on fire again."

"I know." He tucked a loose strand of hair behind her ear. Then took her hand and brought it to his lips. "I have an idea." Kissing her knuckles, he watched with what looked like satisfaction when she sighed over the incredibly romantic gesture.

"I thought we could start at the beginning. Get to know each other again. We'd go real slow, have a good time. Enjoy ourselves."

"How?" she asked suspiciously.

He laughed. "Don't tell me you've forgotten how to have fun. Never mind, I'll have to show you."

She was intrigued, then nervous. "About what you said to me. You know. How you . . ."

"You mean how I love you?"

She nodded, swallowing. "You'll be wanting me to return that sentiment."

"Love is a gift, Jussie," he said with such dignity, she felt like a monster. As if incredibly weary, he turned away, leaned over her desk, and dropped his head between his shoulders.

She swallowed again, because her mouth had suddenly gone dry as cotton. She watched him stretch his shoulders as if they were kinked. "I know it's a gift."

"Do you?" he wondered. "Because you make it sound like an obligation."

"Well, maybe I don't feel obligated," she whispered, butterflies attacking her stomach with what she *did* feel. "Maybe I feel *it* back. A little."

His head whipped up, his eyes fierce. "What?"

"I said maybe I feel it back," she said, lifting her chin and daring him to believe her. "A little."

"Maybe?" His voice was hoarse, thick.

She'd never seen such an intense, yet needy expression. "Yeah. Sort of."

"Jussie," he said warningly.

"All right." She garnered her courage. "I think . . . I do."

Okay, Mitch thought, this was far too important to misunderstand. Heart pumping, he pushed away from the desk and came back to her, careful to maintain his distance. He had to, or he'd drag her closer and shake her until she told him what he was so desperate to hear. "You think you do *what*?"

A pent-up breath of air puffed out her cheeks. She bit her lip. "I think maybe I love you." Her shoulders sagged. "A little. Sort of. Maybe."

Blood roared in his ears, his knees went weak with relief. Cupping her face so he could see her lovely eyes, he tipped her head up. He saw nervousness and more than a little anxiety. "I'm rushing you," he murmured. "Again."

"I just wanted you to know." She licked her lips. She brought her hands up to grip his wrists. "I want to be honest."

For the first time all day—hell, for the first time in two years, his smile came from his heart. "Honesty's good, Jussie. But I want you to be sure. No matter how much I rant, just take your time." He stepped back to prove it. "I don't want this to make you miserable."

To his horror, her eyes filled.

"No, baby, don't cry," he begged. "God, I'm sorry."

"I don't want you to think I'm unhappy you're back," she said. "I'm not. But I'm so confused."

He swiped a tear off her cheeks with his thumb. "We're married. What's so confusing?"

Her lips curved a little. "Basically, you mean why can't we just jump into bed and get on with this marriage?"

Now he laughed at her. "Well, basically, yes."

She laughed despite her tears, and shook her head. "Oh, Mitch. It sounds so ungrateful, but I'm just . . . frightened. Of you. And me. And what I feel. Please—" Her voice cracked. "Please, just be patient with me. I—I want to do what you said. I want to start over. From the beginning."

"As in you living somewhere other than with me?"

"For now."

No, he wouldn't do this. "You were nearly killed yesterday, Jussie. Not to mention the phone calls, the faxes with the cryptic warnings. I heard what you said about Mitzy, and I'll check that out next. I'm on the mayor thing as we speak, and he just might be blowing steam, but you can't possibly believe I'll let you go home alone."

"Devlin's there."

"I'm where?" Devlin, smiling and holding an early edition of the *Daily News*, walked in. "Hey, guys. Check out this great article I did on . . ." His smile faded at the obvious thick tension. "Geez. Are you two at it again?" He shook his head. "You know, the staff is beginning to talk. First you get caught in the storage closet, then you can't speak in public without making goo-goo eyes at each other. And that's not counting the rumor about your office the other night—"

Mitch made a choking sound that sounded suspiciously like laughter, but when Justine glared at him, he swallowed it.

"What do you mean, a rumor about my office the other night?" she demanded, whirling on her brother.

His smile was smug. "You're not going to make me tell you about the birds and the bees now, are you?"

Oh, no. Had she made a noise, or cried out? She'd experienced the most explosive climax of her life right there on the couch, going deaf, dumb, and blind in the process. She might have screamed for all she knew. "Devlin," she said through her teeth. "*No one* was here that night. And no one could have possibly seen Mitch and me in the closet—" She stopped and felt herself turn beet red. "Oh, this is so unprofessional." She turned on Mitch when he laughed. "And it's all *your* fault."

He leaned casually back against the desk, completely unconcerned. "If you'd have listened to me in the first place, I wouldn't have had to lock you in there."

Devlin gaped. "Locked her in?"

"Never mind!" Justine groaned, miserable. "This is going to require massive damage control. But I'm too tired tonight. I'm out of here, guys."

"Wait."

Mitch caught her arm as she buzzed by, and before she could blink, she found herself with her back to the door and one hundred and seventy-five pounds of dangerous male holding her there.

"You can't go alone."

She resented the tone, even though she knew he was right. "Of course I can."

"What the hell's going on?" Devlin asked, straightening.

"I think Jussie was the target of that shooter," Mitch said, his gaze never lifting from her.

Devlin went white. "The drive-by in the parking lot?"

"That's the one. And the death threats have increased." Mitch lifted an eyebrow, daring Justine to contradict him.

"What death threats?" Devlin demanded. "What's going on?"

"Nothing—" Justine said, pushing Mitch away.

Mitch didn't budge. "Tell him, Jussie."

"It's *nothing*, I told you. Look, I'm the editor of a daily, I get things like this all the time. It's some crackpot trying to scare me, that's all."

Mitch swore softly.

"Is that 'dammit,' no, it's not a crackpot," Devlin asked Mitch. "Or is that 'dammit,' my sister is being an idiot?"

"Both," Mitch declared fervently.

"Oh, please," Jussie muttered. She opened her purse, pulled out her keys. "The crackpot's name is Mitzy Thompson, and as far as I'm concerned, she's harmless." She turned to the door.

"Yeah," Mitch said, standing in her way. "As a snake."

Devlin narrowed his eyes and moved closer, adding his slight bulk to Mitch's. "What the hell is this about Mitzy?"

"Nothing. Forget it," Justine insisted.

But her brother was as stubborn as she. "Is that story you ran about the mayor's questionable tie to Q-Vac earning you death threats?"

Mitch nearly swallowed his tongue. "What? What do you know about Q-Vac?"

Devlin looked at him, clearly puzzled over his low, urgent tone. "Not much, as a sportswriter."

"Q-Vac is this huge corporation on the coast, about thirty miles from here," Justine said, frowning at Mitch. "You must remember it. They're the largest tire manufacturer in the western United States—"

"I know what they make," Mitch said. In fact, he knew just about everything about the place—including how many federal agents had been sent in to see why the place had been allowed to dump nearly one hundred times the allotted amount of pollution into the air. He knew this because that fateful day at his first fed meeting, he and one other agent had witnessed one of those agents on the take for Q-Vac. That other agent with him had been murdered for what he'd seen, and Mitch would have been next.

It'd been the catalyst for all that had happened, commencing his next two years of hell. "Wait a minute. Q-Vac is the corporation you alluded to in your articles?" His voice was rough, his heart thundering.

"Well . . ." Justine glanced quickly at Devlin. "Yes. I named them yesterday."

And he'd been so busy breaking into the FBI's computer, he hadn't read the paper.

Q-Vac. Dammit, it was all falling into place. One agent had been killed and another had died because of a mixture of his own greed and the corporation's corruption. Mitch had spent two years of his life a virtual prisoner of the government, hoping to keep the two people he cared about most in the entire world safe. Devlin and Jussie.

They were both looking expectantly at him. How did he explain this? "Justine," he said slowly, dread welling. "Tell me about the mayor and Q-Vac."

"They supposedly donated heavily to his election campaign in order to influence certain environmental laws. He denied it, since as a member of the board of Q-Vac, it would be illegal to take in what he did."

"The mayor is on the payroll there." Mitch closed his eyes. How had Hopkins missed this?

Looking concerned at the strangled tone in his voice, Justine nodded. "I think so, though it has never been proven. But now the mayor's decided to run for Congress next year, and the rumors are recirculating. Especially with those new radical pollution laws in the referendum at the same election." Now she glanced at Devlin, her gaze hooded.

"Tell me," Mitch said, holding his breath, *knowing* she was holding back again. "Tell me the rest."

"I've never been able to prove it. Not without a doubt. But Devlin provided the source."

Devlin made a protesting noise and Mitch looked at him.

"He won't name him," she said quietly, watching her brother. "But I know whoever he is he must have the proof I need to bring the mayor down."

Mitch's stomach clenched, aware for the first time how much she'd put on the line over this story. Including her own life, damn her. Didn't she realize how dangerous this was? "The warnings said 'back off'."

"Yes, both of them," she agreed. "And I thought it must be Mayor Thompson, at first. But then Mitzy said something to me today that nearly echoed the warning word for word. I don't know why she'd care what I wrote on the father she loves to hate, but it's a possibility."

"It's a good possibility," Mitch agreed.

"No," Devlin insisted urgently. "That's not it. It's not her."

"Given her suspension, it's got to be." Jussie studied him, clearly surprised, as Mitch was, at his vehemence. "Unless you know something you'd like to share, Dev."

He shook his head.

Her sister remained positive. "Either way, it's just a threat. As angry as the mayor and his daughter obviously are, I don't believe either of them could really hurt me. It's just a scare tactic."

Too close, Mitch thought, watching Devlin's pale, nervous expression. He felt shaky when he thought about how many times in the past two years Jussie could have innocently incited this exact situation. "There were messages on your desk from Mitzy. What about? The articles on her father?"

Her eyes went unfriendly. "Those were my personal telephone messages, Mitch."

"Yes, and you've been *personally* threatened," he reminded her. "What did she want, Jussie?"

"Devlin, actually." She let out a little self-mocking laugh. "Until *you* came into town."

Devlin turned a bright red.

"Why is she interested in me?" Mitch demanded.

Justine rolled her eyes. "Have you looked at your pretty mug in the mirror lately?"

Mitch would have liked to explore that slightly defensive tone to her voice, since it suggested jealousy and a whole host of feelings he definitely wanted to know about.

"Buying that huge house didn't help," Justine said evenly, though her gaze was plainly curious. "She's been salivating."

"So she is or isn't upset about what you wrote on her father?"

"Isn't." Devlin shook his head. "There's no love lost there. It's not her, guys. It can't be."

"Why was she calling, then?" Mitch asked.

Devlin hesitated, then shrugged. "Maybe since she's suspended, she knows something that she wants the paper to report. Maybe."

Mitch started to speak, but Justine stopped him with a hand to his arm. She eyed her brother speculatively. "Spill it," she said quietly.

Devlin turned away to pace the length of the office. "I'm just saying that maybe she's not the bad guy here. That's all."

"No one said she was for sure." But Mitch had thought it, more than once.

Justine just looked at her brother, then let out a sound of amused regret.

Devlin shifted, avoided her gaze. "What?"

"You didn't."

Now he crossed his arms, and Mitch watched with some amusement as Justine goaded someone other than himself for a change.

"I don't know what you're talking about," Devlin claimed stoutly.

"You did!" Justine clapped a hand to her mouth, but a laugh escaped. "You slept with her. Oh, Dev. That's so . . . desperate."

"No, *desperate* is knocking it out in the stock closet!"

"You don't know what you're talking about." But her eyes slid guiltily to the couch behind them and Devlin hooted.

"And your couch!" he added, doubling over while he laughed, slapping his thigh. "Talk about *desperate.* Ah . . . sorry, Mitch," he added politely. "No offense meant."

"No offense taken," said Mitch with the straightest face he could manage. "But just because we know Mitzy has, uh . . . excellent taste in men"—he broke off to give a mock glare to Jussie when she scoffed—"doesn't mean much in the way of her character. Unless someone here knows something I don't?" He looked at Devlin.

He was still red to his ears.

"Devlin?" Justine looked at him hopefully. "Tell me it was just a quick case of lust. That you didn't fall for that bossy, nosy, interfering—what?" she demanded of the suddenly silently-shaking-with-mirth Mitch. "*What?*"

"*I'm* the one that fell for a bossy, nosy, interfering woman, and her name isn't Mitzy—"

"Oh, you're funny."

But it wasn't funny at all, and suddenly Mitch knew he couldn't take a chance, not with either of them. "Listen," he said quickly. "I need both of you to do something for me, and it's going to take total and complete trust."

Devlin, frowning, nodded without hesitation.

Jussie, bless her stubborn, ornery heart, only stared at him, glowering. "What?"

"Jussie." He struggled for patience. "Please. *Please* promise me you'll do what I ask, no questions." He stared her down for a painfully long minute, absorbing her frustration. Blind faith didn't come easily for her. "Please."

"Fine," she said grumpily, *finally*, with a loud huff.

"Good." He drew an uneven breath. "I'm going to need your source, Dev. No other way to go about it. Once we have physical evidence, and run a front-page article, the scoop will be out once and for all. There'll be no reason for whomever to continue the threats against

Jussie, since hopefully, they'll not only be in jail, but the mayor will be ruined. Right?"

"But I can't promise my source will reveal their identity," Devlin protested.

"He has to," Mitch said. "Because we may not get so lucky on the next little parking-lot session." He could tell by Devlin's sudden loss of color that he'd made his point. "Is it a plan?"

Devlin nodded. Jussie, looking thoughtful, nodded as well.

"Good." Mitch knew this was the tricky part. "Until then, the two of you are leaving town. I have a cabin in the mountains, about two hours from here."

"A cabin?" Jussie stared at him.

He had no time to tell her Hopkins had given him the cabin after his wife died, saying he could never go back. Mitch had kept it for Jussie and himself, but he'd never imagined taking her there under these circumstances. "It's remote. Safe. We'll go there."

"Why? For how long? This is ridiculous—" Justine started, only to break off mid-sentence at Mitch's upheld hand.

"You promised," he said softly.

"We'll go," Devlin said firmly, ignoring Justine's outraged exclamation. "But you can't really think Mitzy is responsible for this. It's too farfetched. Too desperate."

"I'm sorry, Dev." Mitch didn't miss Dev's clear concern. Whether Jussie wanted to see it or not, things between her brother and Mitzy had gone further than he'd admitted.

"You're wrong about this," Devlin said slowly. "But

right about needing to go until the proof is out and the mayor fingered. Jussie needs to be gone."

"Oh, nice. *Both* of you speak for me now."

They both scowled at her and she relented.

"Fine. We'll go. But not until after tomorrow night's Christmas party for the paper."

Mitch started to protest, but she went on quickly, "We can't go before then, it'll look strange. Besides, if she wanted me dead that badly, wouldn't I already be so?"

"She's got a point," her brother said. "Besides, you'll get an up-front and personal view of her at the party. Mitzy's sort of my, ah . . . date."

"Oh, Dev." Jussie moaned. "Anyone but her, *please*."

Mitch's thoughts raced while brother and sister bickered. Worrying himself sick over Jussie for another twenty-four hours weighed against the appeal of keeping her near him. And no matter what Devlin and Jussie thought, he could practically taste the danger. "All right," he said finally. "We'll wait until tomorrow night. We'll run the article the next morning, and you'll both be far gone."

"Are you sure we have to leave at all?" Jussie set her big blue eyes on him hopefully. "What if I just stay in my office and work? You can guard the door—"

"It has to be this way. We have no idea how far you can push him. Or her." Mitch went to her, hauled her close, and hugged her tight until she squirmed to be free.

He didn't give a damn about her fretting about what Devlin saw between them. "For me," he whispered. "I need to hold you."

Just that simply, she went lax. Tentatively, her arms

squeezed around him. Relief, love, and fear mingled with fierce intensity.

Devlin stood facing the window with his hands jammed in his pockets, giving them as much privacy as he could within the small office.

"I wanted to start slow," Justine whispered against Mitch's neck. "Going away with you *isn't* slow."

"There's just no other way. I won't risk you. Either of you. Don't ask me to."

Her huge eyes blinked at him, filled with things that made him ache. "Mitch . . ." In a shocking but touching display of public affection, she cupped his face, then kissed him softly.

"I love you," he said simply, unable to keep it in.

Her eyes welled. "Don't give up on me," she whispered. "Please, don't. I couldn't stand it if you did."

"I won't. Ever."

She nodded, swallowing hard before admitting, "I'm scared."

Against her hair, he murmured, "It's the only way, Jussie. Please, baby, this is the only way."

"The only way to what?"

"To keep you alive long enough for you to decide you can't live without me."

FOURTEEN

Why had he agreed to this Christmas party? Mitch wondered as he stalked his bedroom looking for a tie.

From outside came the unmistakable signs of a brewing storm. Heavy winds. Driving rain hitting the windows.

From the bathroom came the unidentifiable sounds of a woman doing . . . well, whatever it was a woman did to get ready. Something clunked onto the tile. Water ran. Clothing rustled.

Most of his disgruntlement about dressing up died right then as a wave of warm contentment rolled over him.

Jussie. He could picture her in there, brushing her silky hair until it shone, putting on that peach gloss that tasted so good, pulling up her stockings . . . God.

His tie wasn't working.

From inside the bathroom came a muffled oath and he grinned. Jussie was having trouble as well.

She'd given in gracefully when he'd refused to leave

her side, but he had the feeling it was due more to her fear from her latest barrage of threats by phone and fax than to her wanting to be with him.

Judging by the paleness of her complexion at the end of the day, he figured he shouldn't delude himself—she was preoccupied, and it wasn't with thoughts of him. That would come, he promised himself. For now, it just felt good to know she was close.

And that she loved him. Sort of, maybe, a little.

His grin spread. She loved him all right, and it was enough that *he* knew it. For now.

In the bathroom, there was sudden silence, and he wondered what she was doing, thinking. Was she nervous about tonight?

By this time two days from now, it'd all be over. Jussie had secretly written the last article in the mayor saga. After the party, Devlin's still-unnamed source had promised to provide the proof to go along with that article. It would run tomorrow morning.

Because of this, and the possibility of immediate retribution, Mitch planned on taking Jussie to the cabin that night, directly after the party. Devlin would meet them there with his source, since he felt adamant that this person might also suffer the consequences.

Mitch had talked to Hopkins about the recent turn of events, and the two of them had decided to keep the protective tail on both Justine and Devlin until the end, though Hopkins maintained he didn't believe the danger was real. He thought it likely the mayor and his daughter were merely bluffing. They figured two days at the most, and everything would be back to normal.

Then Mitch would ask Jussie to wear her rings again. Grimacing into the mirror over his dresser, he worked his tie, thinking he'd probably strangle in it before the night was over.

"I don't know why these damn parties are always so formal," he grumbled when he heard Jussie step out of his bathroom behind him. "I can't stand wearing a tux—" He caught sight of her in the mirror and his words simply dried up in his throat.

She wore black velvet. Off-the-shoulder, body-hugging, hip-flaring, soft, crushed velvet that made him ache to touch her. She'd left her hair down to sweep in a curtain of burnished gold and fire over her shoulders.

Her eyes shimmered with a heat that had his knees weak.

When he continued to stare at her stupidly, she smiled a little nervously. Walking up to him, she gently brushed his ineffectual hands away from his tie and took over the job with quick, competent movements.

He finally found his voice. "God, Jussie."

Tipping her head back to look at him, her little smile faded. In the black tux, with his dark hair falling over his forehead, and that fiercely intense expression on his rugged face, he looked so magnificent. So tough. So tender. *So hers.* "You're so gorgeous," she said without thinking.

The quick, crooked smile was tinged with pleased embarrassment. "That was my line." He drew a slow finger down her throat, across a bare collarbone.

"I mean it." She clasped her hands behind her back to keep them off him. "But it has nothing to do with what you look like."

"Thanks," he said with a little laugh. "I think."

"What I'm trying to say is . . ." She licked her lips nervously. Her stomach clenched. "Ah . . ."

"Are you all right?" He took her face in his hands, inspecting her. "You're not, dammit."

Because it felt so good, and because she felt so needy, she leaned into him. She rested her head on his chest, sighing when he wrapped his arms around her.

"You try to be too strong," he said huskily, running his big, warm hands over her back. His roughened but gentle fingers skimmed lightly over the edge of the dress, flirting with her bare skin until a delicious shiver racked her. "Too in control. I wish you'd share more of yourself with me. I . . . really need you to."

"I know." It shamed her that she'd held back, when he'd given her everything. Closing her eyes, ignoring the gut-tightening emotion bouncing off her nerves, she took the plunge. "I love you, Mitch."

His hands stilled for an instant before diving into her hair to draw her head back. "Finally," he breathed as his mouth covered hers, giving her with that one kiss far more than any soft words of love could have done. His voice was thick with emotion. "*Finally*."

It was different, this kiss, and Justine felt it immediately. The tender way he held and stroked her, the gentle way he moved his mouth over hers—she simply melted. It was every bit as wonderful, as delicious, as wicked as ever, but it went deeper, so much beyond what they'd shared in the heat of the moment in her office.

This kiss said, *You have my heart, you share my soul*. It said, *This is forever*.

But then he lifted his head and set her away from him. And though his hands were slow to leave her, and his breathing was uneven, he shot her his trademark crooked grin. "Any more of that, and we'll be late." As his gaze ran down her once more he shook his head and whistled low. "*Very* late."

"Late's okay," she murmured, reaching for him, but he just laughed and held her off.

"No, sweetheart. I meant, if we don't go now, I'm likely to mess up that drop-dead-gorgeous dress."

"I don't care if you do," she assured him, trying to press up against his body. She wanted more, now.

"*I* care." He groaned when her breasts brushed against his chest. "I want you so badly, I'm shaking with it, but I don't want to be worried about your pretty hair or smearing your makeup." He lowered his voice, skimming his fingers over her neck, lower.

"Just a kiss, then," Justine begged.

"One won't be enough. And when I take that dress off you tonight—which I'm going to—it's *not* going back on."

Heat flooded her face, her mouth dropped open. Her eyes were wide, wild, and . . . expectant. "Oh."

Quite satisfied with his world, Mitch leaned forward, whispering in her ear *exactly* what he planned to do to her once he got the black velvet off.

Her eyes glazed over, her fingers dug into his shoulders. "Tell me again why we have to go to the party?"

Typically, Justine dreaded parties. She felt like a fish out of water. She loathed the limelight. She hated small talk. And she despised feeling as if she was on display.

All reasons to wish the evening to a quick end.

Across the room, Mitch turned from his conversation with Devlin and smiled at her, his eyes dancing with love and affection and passion. Every rational thought flew right out of her head.

Then she remembered his whispered promises about the evening still ahead, and blushed. He lifted a suggestive eyebrow and she blushed even more.

"Oh, *please*," Mitzy said as she sidled up to Justine. "If you're going to keep the most gorgeous man in Heather Bay to yourself, and then make eyes at each other all evening, at least have the decency to get a hotel room."

More intrigued than frightened, Justine studied the other woman. She felt certain Mitzy had been the one trying to scare her, but with Mitch only across the room, she felt safe enough. "Jealous?"

"No need." Mitzy laughed, but it sounded flat. "Not when every other man's tongue is hanging out over me."

Justine looked at the glittery, sequined, short silvery number Mitzy had chosen for the evening, and had to admit she looked fantastic. "I'm constantly amazed at how you fit through the door with that ego of yours."

When Mitzy didn't respond with the usual quip, Justine narrowed her eyes. It was one thing to make snide remarks when Mitzy returned each barb with a sharper one. But to pick on someone who wasn't up for it filled her with unease. "Mitzy?"

But the mayor's daughter was staring across the room, a look of such intent emotion on her face, such hunger and longing, it took Justine's breath away.

But all that air clogged in her throat when she realized *who* Mitzy was watching.

Devlin.

How many men's hearts had Mitzy destroyed this year alone? The number was staggering. "Stay away from him," Justine said in a low voice, angry and suddenly very afraid. "It's bad enough what you're doing to me, but he's done nothing to you. *Nothing.*"

Mitzy only looked amused. "And what the hell do you think I'm doing to *you?*"

"Come on. 'Back off or die'? Couldn't you have come up with something scarier than that?"

Mitzy went still, and she searched Justine's face carefully. "I swear I don't know what you're talking about."

"Yeah, right." Justine lowered her voice as a couple from marketing walked by. "Just keep away from Devlin." She forced a smile and wave for Beth in accounting. "*I mean it.*"

Mitzy stayed absolutely frozen for another second. Then, slowly, she relaxed. Just defrosted right in front of Justine's eyes. Never missing a beat, Mitzy moved her hips slightly to the beat of the music, then raised her flute in a toast made into a challenge by her words. "Try to make me," she said sweetly, lifting the glass to her lips for a long draft of champagne.

She handed Justine the empty glass and walked away.

Justine glanced at Devlin, who from across the room was watching her with an inscrutable expression. Slowly, he shifted his gaze from his sister to Mitzy, who'd stopped to flirt with the senior news editor.

At the sight of the longing and hunger in *his* eyes, she groaned.

It was going to be a long night. As if sensing her thoughts, the deliriously upbeat Christmas music revved up. Someone cheered. The sounds of merriment came from every direction.

Still, Devlin watched Mitzy. And Justine watched him.

"You can't protect him forever," Mitch said softly as he came up behind her.

Justine sighed when he wrapped a strong arm around her waist and pulled her back against him. It shouldn't feel so good to have him to lean on. It shouldn't feel so right to know he was there for her, no matter what. But it did, and she was sick and tired of analyzing it when all she wanted to do was feel, take . . . give.

She let herself sag back, soaking up his strength, his love. He made a noise low in his throat; half groan, half laugh.

"Did you know?" he whispered in her ear as he crowded her in the most pleasant of ways. "That from this angle I can see straight down that dress?"

Just the rough, gravelly tone, mixed with his warm breath on her skin, had heat pooling between her legs, her nipples tightening. From his vantage point, he had a great view of her reaction, and she felt his muffled groan vibrate through her.

It had been a wordless sound, but she knew exactly what he meant. "Mitch." She felt reckless. *Desperate*. "Let's go."

He still stood behind her, and he slid his jaw over her hair, then bent slightly to put his lips to her temple. "Soon." Then he whispered a reminder in her ear what would happen when "soon" arrived.

Justine was thankful that no one seemed to notice them, because she could barely keep her eyes from drifting shut, her knees from giving out.

Mitch urged her even closer, until her bottom had nestled against the tops of his thighs, until she could feel what she'd done to him.

She made a little gasp of her own, which turned into a moan when his teeth tugged on her ear.

"Smile, sweetheart," he said, laughing softly and spreading his fingers possessively over her belly. A flash made them both blink. "I think we just made the social page for tomorrow's paper."

"Hmm. That's *not* all that's going to hit the paper tomorrow." A surge of adrenaline hit her, made her grin widely in anticipation of her scoop. "I hope to God that Devlin's source comes through." Without the proof, she and the paper would be in big trouble.

Hope and the promise of relief from the strain of the threats made her giddy. Despite the fact that the music around them had slowed, softened, and that people were slow-dancing, she jumped a little jig. Whirling in Mitch's arms, she faced him, still grinning. "I feel free," she said, then laughed. "Oh, that sounds so corny, but it's true."

His arms tightened on her as his smile faded slowly. Hungrily, his gaze roamed her face. "I haven't seen you this happy in far too long," he said in a voice husky with emotion. "It looks good on you."

She could only stare at him as she realized.

"What?" He cupped her face. "What is it?"

A shaky laugh escaped her. "It's *you*," she whispered, her eyes shining. "Mitch, it's not the prospect of the scoop. Or even having the threats stop." She gripped his jacket and leaned close. "It's you. *You're* the one making me so happy."

His heart stopped, then kick-started. Biting back the urge to kiss her long and senseless right there, he slowly drew her into his arms, cradled her there, then savored the feel of her body pressed against his.

They stood there like that for a long moment, swaying slightly to the music. Mitch knew the exact second it happened, when the embrace changed. The slight dance movements became erotic. Everywhere their bodies touched sent off little shock waves.

Justine tipped backward to stare at him, and the connection was instant. Eyes smoldering, she sent him a naughty grin, pressing her hips against his erection, laughing when his eyes crossed with lust.

"Let's go," he said, his voice strained.

She laughed again. "I thought you said 'soon.'"

"Soon's arrived."

They made it to the parking lot, drenched from the rain, and laughing like two little kids. Inside Mitch's car, they fell together in the front seat, still grinning like fools. He scooted the seat back as far as it would go, making more room, then pulled her onto his lap with a naughty grin.

"I'm f-freezing." Justine stuttered, throwing her wet limbs around Mitch's neck.

He yelped at the shock of cold skin, then paid her back by snaking his equally frozen hands up her thighs and under her dress.

"Mitch—" She gasped, sucking in her breath when his clever, greedy, icy fingers found the firm, bare skin above her thigh-high stockings. She sighed when he lifted her over him to straddle his legs. While his hands cupped and gently squeezed her bottom, his lips went to work on her throat.

Her head fell back. He tried to move her closer, and banged his leg on the gearshift, making him swear.

"It's like high school." She laughed breathlessly, leaning over him to kiss him. "Let's make out, Mitch."

Her hair dripped over his face. Her cold fingers sank into his hair. His bones were icy, but none of that mattered. Not when he had Jussie in his arms, on his lap, and looking at him with those incredibly huge, warm eyes. "Come here," he said, pulling her down for a long, deep kiss that stirred even more needs.

She tasted so good, felt so perfect as she straddled him with surprising ease. But kisses were no longer enough.

"More," she whispered, echoing his thoughts as she wiggled enticingly on his lap. "God, Mitch. More." Then, without waiting for him, she went to work on his buttons, spreading his shirt wide as she went. Her damp hair trailed over his chest as she bent to her task, and when her lips connected with one of his nipples, he groaned.

"Good?" she asked.

"Mmmmm. Jussie . . . wait," he said hoarsely when she slid to the floor at his feet, her tongue swirling down his belly. His muscles leaped and tensed. "Let me drive us home."

"No. Now." She spread openmouthed kisses over his body while her fingers worked the fastenings of his trousers.

"Jussie, sweetheart, someone might . . . God—" he whispered explosively when her fingers found him. "Jussie . . . wait—"

She interrupted the thought with her mouth, and kissed him until he was too far gone to protest. Her hands, those busy hands took him right to the brink, but still he managed to gasp out, "Someone might see us—" His words ending on a groan when she tugged the black velvet of her dress down, down, exposing herself to her waist.

The hell with it, he decided as he urged her back on his lap. He dipped forward to take a tight, budded nipple into his mouth. After all, he reasoned to himself a bit desperately, they were at the end of the lot, and the windows had completely fogged over. The fierce little sounds she made as he suckled her drove him to the very edge. She whispered his name, begging for more, and to the tune of the driving rain and the rustle of the leather beneath him, he gave it.

It took but one tug to have the snug, short skirt of her dress up to her hips. Another, and her wispy little black panties gave way, allowing him the view he'd been dreaming about all night. She was hot, trembly, and ready for him. Within minutes his fingers brought her to a first, shuddering orgasm that nearly triggered his own.

"Now," she whispered, rising up and guiding him to her. "I want to feel you inside me. Now." But she hesitated, poised over the very tip of him, and sent him a smile filled with everything he'd ever wanted. "I love you," she said in a soft, fierce voice, and started to sink down on him.

His hands on her hips stopped her descent. In a haze, he barely managed to groan out, "Wait." Frustration bit into him. "I don't have any protection with me."

Her smile turned watery as love overflowed. "I know," she whispered. "Mitch, I don't want to be protected. Not from you."

Befuddled by passion, he needed a minute to realize what she was offering, but when he did, his heart simply burst. "Jussie, are you sure?"

"Yeah. Is that okay with you?" she asked in return,

and he found he wanted to laugh and cry and make love all at the same time.

"Yeah," he said on a choked moan when she slowly rocked her hips once over his. His own eyes unnaturally bright, he met her gaze straight on. "I love you. I love you with everything I've got."

Wild joy and love surged through her with his softly spoken words, and she impaled herself with one quick motion of her hips. He cried out, and she thought she probably did, too, but she could no longer hear anything but the blood pumping through her heart. Heaven, she thought. It was absolutely heaven when he filled her. They both gasped with the pleasure of it. Content to savor the thickness of him inside her forever, she went still.

His fingers squeezed her hips gently, urging her to rock against him. "You feel incredible," he whispered against her throat. He tried to arch his hips to bring himself more deeply within her, but he was hampered by the tight confines of the car. "Jussie . . . baby, I can't . . . you've got to—ah, yes," he groaned when she raised her hips a little.

"We ought to make this a regular outing," she said, slowly moving up the long length of him. His mouth found her breasts again, and he hummed her approval. "Don't you think?"

"Hmm? Yeah," he mumbled around the flesh in his mouth. "Regular."

"We could . . ." Her voice faltered when his hands slipped beneath her bottom to urge her to move again. "We could try the backseat next time. How about that?"

Where their bodies were joined, he touched her

lightly, and she jerked responsively. "Backseat," he agreed, trying to arch his hips again.

"Because we'd have—" she began, only to end on a moan when his fingers stroked her slow and sure, light and teasing. "More room back there."

"Jussie, sweetheart, shut up and take me. I'm dying here."

She laughed huskily and moved on him. His hands helped, encouraged, roamed over her, stroking, smoothing over her breasts, her belly, her bottom. Her breathing quickened, panted, and she rested her forehead to his. "Oh, Mitch—" But that was all she managed before she shattered in his arms.

In the next breath he shattered in hers, coming to an explosive release that shook his entire body.

Home, he thought as he clasped her close and shuddered.

He'd finally come home.

FIFTEEN

Mitch pulled the car through the lot, still grinning. "I can't see a damn thing," he said, swiping at the window as he slowly drove past the building.

Justine glanced at his ridiculously pleased smile and had to laugh. "Just don't get us pulled over. I don't want to explain that your idiotic grin has nothing to do with alcohol."

Mitch's amusement faded at the sight of Devlin standing alone in the night, waving his hand to get their attention. He pulled over and rolled down the window.

"Hey, Dev, what's up?"

Devlin leaned in the window a bit and handed a bulging brown envelope past him to Jussie. "Proof," he said so flatly that her brows creased together in concern.

"Dev?" Her voice was still husky from their love-making. She cleared it. "What's the matter?"

His jaw tightened. "Just take it." But his hand still gripped the envelope, as if he were regretting his decision to give it up.

"Something's wrong," Mitch said. "What is it?"

Devlin's fingers loosened as he let the envelope go. He straightened, jammed his hands in his pockets, and shook his head. "Nothing. It's just . . . nothing."

Justine peered in the package. "Bank statements, yes!" She lowered her excited voice, though the parking lot was empty. "And telephone records. Oh, Dev, this is perfect."

"Other records are in there too," Devlin said. "Are you going to give them to the cops?"

Justine obviously saw the same strain that Mitch did. "You know I have to," she said softly. "Is that a problem?"

"No." He seemed to shrug off his trouble, even managed a smile. "Make merry, sis. Mitch. See you later."

"Wait!" she called as he started to walk away. "When do I meet the source?"

"At the cabin," Devlin said over his shoulder. "We're still meeting there tonight, right?"

Justine glanced at Mitch.

Mitch knew what she wanted. She wanted him to say it was no longer necessary. That there wouldn't be any need to hole away, but he couldn't. He still felt strongly that he needed to get Justine the hell out of here until everything blew over. "Yes, we're going to the cabin."

Justine sighed. "We'll meet you there."

Devlin nodded solemnly and walked off, his shoes squeaking on the wet asphalt.

Justine watched him leave, her expression worried. "Something's wrong."

"I know. It's his source, I think."

"We'll find out tonight, I imagine. I hope he's not scared."

"It's going to be all right." Hopkins had promised to keep a tail on the mayor and his daughter until this was over. He, Mitch, was taking Devlin and Jussie out of town. Things were under control.

She had tucked her feet beneath her on the seat. Her lovely dress wasn't quite as neat as it had been when she'd first put in on, and her hair had gotten hopelessly and adorably tangled in their excitement. She wiggled deeper into her seat, probably for warmth. He knew she hadn't replaced her ripped panties, and just the thought had him hard again.

She visibly shrugged off her melancholy and turned to him. Something in his eyes must have given him away, for her lips curved slowly. "Is it 'soon' again?"

"Oh, yeah," he said, and took her home.

The drive up the mountain was a challenge. The storm had kicked in again, full force. Mitch had the radio on, listening for the road conditions, but he didn't need to hear it to know they might have trouble getting up to the cabin. It'd started to snow lightly, and he could only hope it stayed light because he had no desire to get out and put on chains.

Justine had turned over the evidence to the police with the promise to reveal the source by morning.

A perfect plan. A perfect getaway.

Still, he couldn't shake that feeling. The one he got when things were about to go awry. If only he knew exactly where they were going to go wrong, he could do something about it. *Helpless.* He really hated that feeling.

It didn't take long for him to figure out part of the problem.

Halfway up the mountain, with Jussie sound asleep on the seat beside him, he failed to be able to contact Devlin.

"Dammit." He tapped the car phone absently, wondering why Devlin didn't pick up his cell phone.

Because something's wrong.

He debated turning around, but decided to continue, and dialed Hopkins. "You've got the mayor and Mitzy covered, right?"

"Hello, to you too," said Hopkins grumpily. "You know, for someone's who's supposed to be my best friend, you sure yell at me a lot."

"Just tell me."

"Yeah, yeah, everyone's covered. I promised, didn't I?" Hopkins yawned loudly. "And it looks as if you were right. That award you told me about, the one that Mitzy wants so badly, she's not going to get it if the publicity about her father doesn't stop soon."

Mitch already had motive. He needed proof.

"What the hell time is it anyway?" Hopkins wanted to know.

"Late," Mitch said tersely. He glanced at Jussie. She slept, her chest rising and falling softly with each breath. Her hand was fisted beneath her cheek, and one bent knee rested against his thigh. A rush of fierce protectiveness hit him, and he knew he'd do anything, *anything* at all, to keep her safe.

"I have a bad feeling about this," he said into the phone. "A very bad feeling. Mitzy was at the party when we left, and so was Devlin. Now I can't get him on his cell phone."

That seemed to wake Hopkins up. "We've gone over this. Mitzy's being followed by us, Mitch. Devlin's safe. You've got Justine. Just stop worrying so much and enjoy your time at the cabin."

"But—"

"Trust me," Hopkins said. "I know what I'm doing."

Mitch hung up, then blew out his breath, concentrated on the dark, winding road in front of him. For two years he'd trusted this man implicitly. He'd had to, or die. Somehow, for some reason, it wasn't as easy to let go blindly when it was *Jussie's* life was on the line.

Mitch's anxiety drained when an hour later they drove up the cabin's long driveway and saw Devlin's car there. Beside it, and empty, sat the dark blue sedan.

"Who is that?" Justine asked sleepily, sitting up. She'd changed into jeans and a long-sleeved T-shirt. She pulled on a sweatshirt.

"It's the unit that Hopkins put on Mitzy." Without hesitation, he reached for the gun he had holstered beneath his arm. His backup, strapped to his ankle, was a comforting weight.

Justine's eyes went huge. "What—"

"I love you." He kissed her hard.

"A gun?" she asked. "We're going to need a gun?"

He hadn't mentioned that he'd armed himself to the teeth, that he'd been that way ever since the shooting in the parking lot. As a survival and weapons expert, he didn't believe in being unprepared. "We might," he said calmly. Then, because the fear in her eyes escalated, he kissed her again. "Don't worry. I'm good at this."

"Okay." She took a deep breath. "I'm sure that was supposed to make me feel better."

He pushed her down on the seat. "I'll check it out."

"No way." With amazing strength, she fought him and sat back up. "I'm coming with you." She flipped on her hood, then pulled on the parka she'd stored in the backseat.

The cabin looked dark and still, no movement anywhere. Even with the late hour, it seemed strange. "Yes, you're staying with me," Mitch agreed grimly, because he felt far more afraid to leave her behind where he couldn't help her if she needed him.

The gravel driveway was covered with a thin layer of fresh snow. Their feet crunched as they worked their way to the two other cars.

The A-framed cabin was not as small as Justine had thought at first. Few distinguishing features stuck out in the dark. She could see a pretty picture window, surrounded by an empty planter, but little else. They moved stealthily, slowly around to the back, while Justine gritted her teeth and bit back her urge to cry out for Devlin and run.

The door turned easily in Mitch's hand, and even without light, she sensed his frown. Pushing Justine behind him, he stepped into what she could just barely make out as a kitchen.

Why was there no noise? Why no lights? And why, oh, why had Mitch felt he needed to have his gun out and ready?

Sick with worry, she started to call out to her brother, but Mitch turned and placed his hand over her mouth, holding it there until she nodded with understanding. No talking until they knew what the hell was happening.

And what the hell *was* happening? Why hadn't Devlin come out to greet them? she wondered, trying not to be afraid, trying not to make any noise—difficult when her breath came in little pants. Mitch squeezed her hand encouragingly, then pulled her close to his side, keeping a very welcome, warm arm around her. She felt him look at her, felt him willing his strength to be her strength, and with that came a burst of unbelievably powerful love.

Mitch froze, and at the sight of the tall, imposing, absolutely rigid body Justine loved beyond reason, so obviously prepped for violence, she swallowed hard. Panic unfurled as she realized something was wrong, very, very wrong. "Mitch?" she whispered.

In the dark, he touched her, nothing more than a brief contact of fingers to her cheek, yet it was every bit as soothing as any words would have been.

He reached into a drawer, but a sound behind Justine had the hair rising on her neck.

Someone was standing just behind her.

With a burst of panic, she surged toward Mitch just as he flipped on a flashlight.

Justine gasped.

Mitch swore again.

"Well, how nice of you two lovebirds to join us," Mitzy said in a very quiet voice, a large steel kitchen knife gleaming in her hand.

Mitch yanked Justine behind him, aiming his gun at the mayor's daughter.

Mitzy, eyes more than a little wild, laughed softly.

"Oh, you guys are going to get a very big kick out of this later, trust me."

"Put the knife down," Mitch directed in an unwavering voice of steel. "*Now*, Mitzy."

She laughed, sounding slightly hysterical. Justine had never seen her look anything but one hundred percent put together and on the make. She was *not* so well put together now. Her hair tumbled into her eyes. She was breathing too fast, her body tense and wired.

Her voice shook as she stared at his gun. "Mitch, you've got this—"

"Down," he clipped. He flipped on the lights, making them all blink like owls at the sudden brightness. "Put it down."

"All wrong." Mitzy laughed again, but it ended on what sounded like a sobbing hiccup. "I'm playing some sort of Russian roulette meets hide-and-seek here and you want—"

"My gun outweighs your knife," Mitch said coldly, gesturing to the weapon. "Come on, Mitzy. Cooperate."

"*Cooperate*. I'm a little tired of that word, Mitch," she said with amused regret. "I'm afraid I'm not any good at it anyway."

"Where's Devlin?" Justine demanded, incapable of remaining silent a moment longer. She battled with Mitch as he held her firmly behind him. "What have you done with him? If you've hurt him, I'll—"

"He went to check upstairs."

"Then why the knife?" Mitch asked.

"Shhh." Mitzy glanced quickly over her shoulder at a noise that had Mitch tensing as well. "You damn noisy reporter—"

She broke off suddenly, her head cocked as she listened.

Whatever Mitzy saw coming at her from the dark hallway had her drop the knife with a soft exclamation. With a cry, she threw herself at the figure that materialized, and started to sob.

"Devlin," Justine whispered in shock, just as her brother wrapped his arms around Mitzy. She went completely stiff.

From behind them, another figure emerged out of the dark. The man was of average height, but powerfully built. His face, half in the shadows, half revealed by the flickering candle, was hard, unforgiving, yet completely expressionless.

"I've been waiting for you," he said to Mitch. "You took longer than I thought."

"Hopkins?" Mitch lowered his gun as Devlin moved aside with Mitzy. Relief filled him when he realized it had been *Hopkins* in the other car. "You came? Why?"

Hopkins didn't look at Mitch. Without so much as blinking, he lifted what he had in his hands—a gun—and aimed it at Mitzy.

She screamed. Behind Mitch, Justine gasped.

And for the first time in his life Mitch went blank. Absolutely, mind-numbingly blank. The gun slackened in his own hands. Mitzy, while a definite pain in the ass, hadn't lifted a finger to Hopkins in threat, so he didn't understand why the man he'd trusted so completely was pointing a gun at her. "What the hell—"

Hopkins fired. Devlin bellowed and caught Mitzy as she slumped against him.

"That's for screwing me over," Hopkins said quite calmly as he looked down at Mitzy in disgust. "For sneaking around behind your father's back and dipping your nose in where you had no business being. And for handing over the evidence on us when you should have run like hell." He pointed his gun at her again and smiled coldly. "And this is for what you would have done to me with that knife, my dear girl, if you'd have caught me."

"No." Fury temporarily blinded Mitch. But so had loyalty, dammit, and he wouldn't make that mistake twice. With the speed afforded him by his training, he raised his own gun, just a split second after Hopkins resighted, aiming directly at Justine's head.

SIXTEEN

Justine's eyes were riveted with horror on the scene before her. Mitzy sank to the floor, and Devlin hit his knees beside her, cradling her against him.

Mitch, still holding his gun on Hopkins, didn't budge.

"I'm sorry, Mitch," Hopkins said, his face twisting as if in pain, his gun still in Justine's face. "God, I'm sorry. I didn't want it to be this way. You were supposed to stay out of all this, damn you."

Justine looked up at the genuine tone of sorrow in this insane man's voice. But her eyes immediately whipped closed at the sight of his gun pointing directly at her. Where just a minute ago her bones had been, liquid pooled, and she swayed crazily.

With his free hand, Mitch grabbed her arm. "Jussie," he said very quietly. "Get behind me. Now."

"Don't move," Hopkins said conversationally, his gun level on her. "Not an inch."

It was a standoff, with two guns pointed unwaveringly, one at herself, one at the man Mitch had identified as Hopkins.

Somehow, even with the fear coursing through her, Justine managed to speak to Mitch. "*He's* your connection with the FBI? Your . . . friend?"

Not a muscle flickered as Mitch held himself, and his gun, steady as a rock. "The one and only."

The only sound in the room came from Devlin as he tore off his shirt. Holding Mitzy steady, he placed it hard against her wound, trying to stanch the blood flow. She moaned, and the pain that passed over Devlin's face tore at Justine.

"Hold on, baby," he whispered to her. "Hold on. You're going to be all right, just hold on."

"She pretended to be with us simply to get information. She won't live," Hopkins promised lightly. "I can promise you that."

"Yes, she will." Mitch's smile was cold, and his sharp, piercing gaze never left Hopkins. Some unspoken communication seemed to pass between the two of them. "We're *all* going to live. Some of us more comfortably than others, of course."

Hopkins smiled back, almost kindly. "I won't go to jail. You know that. Now drop your gun, Mitch."

"Take yours off my wife."

He didn't comply, and Justine, staring down the wrong end of the barrel of a gun, felt sick. No one moved, and the tension stretched until she thought she might scream.

"Mitch," Hopkins said, his voice not quite as calm. "Don't make me do this. God, please, don't make me hurt you by shooting her right before your eyes. You know I'll do it."

A thousand emotions rushed through Mitch, rage and betrayal leading the way. His fault, dammit, his fault. Hopkins had popped out of the dark, and it seemed so logical, Mitch had hesitated, passing up his one good, free shot.

Now people were going to die because he hadn't protected them as he'd promised.

"You don't understand!" Hopkins said, beginning to lose some of his cool. Sweat beaded on his forehead. "I didn't want this to happen. I didn't want you to get hurt, Mitch."

There was only one way Hopkins could hurt him now, Mitch thought, watching Jussie out of his peripheral vision. Only one way. "Then put the gun down."

"I thought I could keep you out of this." Hopkins swiped at his forehead with his free hand. "I thought you'd go back to your life and stay safe."

"*You* were taking the kickbacks. And I stayed away from my life, from Jussie, because of you?"

Mitzy moaned again, Devlin swore. Jussie, his sweet brave Jussie, lost the last of her color, and he prayed to God she would faint. It would give him the move he needed to blow away Hopkins.

But Jussie locked her knees, lifted her chin stubbornly, and Mitch knew his wife wasn't about to be cowed.

"What happened to that first agent? The one on the take with you?" Mitch asked, hoping desperately for a distraction. "How did he really die?"

"I had him killed," Hopkins said. "He found out about me. I had to eliminate him before he turned me in."

"And the second agent, the one who was murdered?"

"He worked for me as well," Hopkins admitted sadly. "And he was good too. But his greed did him in. I had to take him out for that, or risk everything."

"You and the mayor did this together. You took bribes from Q-Vac and split them. You did this whole thing while others' lives all around you were destroyed."

"No. The mayor worked for *me*," Hopkins clarified, his gaze still carefully trained on Mitch, prepared for anything. "He took his orders from *me*. We split millions over the past few years. Millions. But he got greedy." Disgust tainted his voice now.

"And Q-Vac got tired of paying you off," Justine guessed.

"Jussie," Mitch warned, his voice steady as he tried to control his nerves. "Don't."

Hopkins didn't seem to mind spilling his guts now that he was in control. "Q-Vac was willing to pay their penalties for the pollution and go on, which means we would have had no leverage at all, but the mayor refused to give up a good thing. He wanted the money to keep coming, and he threatened both me and Q-Vac."

"Then Mitzy offered to come up with proof," Mitch said, "and you were stuck."

"Not stuck exactly," Hopkins said casually. "I killed the good old mayor this morning, then hid his body. He won't be found for a while. Now I work alone again," he said, ignoring the shocked gasps of everyone in the room. "Except, of course, for Mitch here. And you just wouldn't leave it alone, man." He spoke with sincere baffled regret.

Mitch felt sick.

"You just couldn't let it go. I couldn't risk it. In another day you'd have figured it out by yourself and come for me."

"You were threatening my wife," Mitch said through his teeth. "What did you expect me to do?"

"That was the mayor, not me." Hopkins shook his head sadly. "He just wouldn't let those articles slide off his back, even when there was absolutely no proof. But then his daughter decided to help the cause and turn us in. Unfortunate for everyone."

"What now?" Mitch wanted to know.

"That's a little tricky," Hopkins said in a kind, fatherly sort of voice. His gun never left Jussie's face as he stepped around Mitzy and came closer. "I really want you to understand, want you to believe I didn't want it to be this way. I care about you, Mitch. I really do. You're the closest thing to a best friend I ever had." He never stopped watching Mitch intently as he came closer, then closer still. He was well aware of Mitch's strength, and obviously didn't want to come within arm's reach.

Devlin shifted slightly behind Hopkins's back, and slowly, his gaze steady on Hopkins, he reached out for the forgotten knife.

"Move away from him, now," Hopkins said to Justine while keeping his gaze on Mitch's. "Do it now, I'm sure you don't want to die yet."

Justine's eyes widened, and she tried to pull away from Mitch, but he wouldn't let her go. Just one clear shot, he promised himself, and Hopkins would be dead.

"No!" Mitzy screamed suddenly, and with a burst of energy, she surged up to a sitting position, grabbed the knife from Devlin, and flung it hard.

Hopkins whirled around just in time to take it in his chest.

SEVENTEEN

Hours later Hopkins was confirmed dead. The police and the FBI's questions had been answered, for now.

Devlin, Justine, and Mitch sat in the hospital waiting room holding hands.

Time crept by.

Finally, Devlin stood up. "Surgery should have been over by now."

Justine went to him, heart thick and heavy in her throat. She hugged him tightly. "Oh, Dev. Why didn't you tell me how much she meant to you? What she'd done for us?"

He held himself stiffly a moment before caving in and wrapping his arms around her. "I don't know. For so long it's been just us, Jus. And you know how Mitzy is . . . all show and talk. It took me a long time to trust her, to realize it was just a front to cover her fear and loneliness." He squeezed his eyes shut and buried his face in Justine's hair. "She cared for me, and let me know right away. And she never faltered, not once, even when I wasn't always kind."

"Dev," she whispered, holding on, wishing she could do more. Her own guilt swamped her. How many times had she taken Mitzy at face value, refusing to see what had been in front of her the entire time? "Dev, if she cares as much as you say, she understands."

"I know. That's what makes it so hard. She just waited for me to love her back. She helped us so much, and now . . ." His voice cracked.

"And now," Justine said with a little sob, "you'll tell her exactly how you feel when she wakes up."

"What if—"

"She'll be all right," Mitch said quietly. He stood, clamped his hand down on Devlin's shoulder, then pushed closer and enclosed the both of them in a bear hug.

The three of them stayed that way a long moment, gaining strength from each other. Then Mitch lifted his head and looked at Justine.

Her already aching heart took yet another beating when she saw the stress and pain in his own watery gaze. He'd said practically nothing for hours, and she knew he was overwhelmed by senseless guilt.

She'd never forget the look on his face when Hopkins had fallen, the knife sticking out of his stout chest. Nor how he'd looked when Hopkins had died in his arms right there on the cabin floor.

Bleak. Betrayed.

He'd been through so much, Jussie thought, aching. His wide shoulders had carried the burden of strength and responsibility for long enough.

Not this time, she vowed. *She* would be the strong one, allowing him to need her as much as she needed him. Reaching for his hand, she smiled through her tears as he grabbed onto her.

They all jerked around when the surgeon came out, face wreathed in smiles. "She's going to be all right," he said immediately. "The bullet was lodged behind her collarbone, but it's clear now." He looked at Devlin. "She wants you, but technically, since you're not family, it's against the rules."

Devlin's eyes flashed. "I'm going to be her family, as soon as she'll let me."

"That's just what I figured, son," the surgeon said with a kind smile. "That's just what I figured. Let's go."

"Jussie," Mitch said hoarsely when they were alone.

The low, urgent tone startled her. Pain and remorse shimmered in his dark green eyes. It was bad, was her only thought. "No," she said quickly, her heart hammering. *"No way."*

A reluctant smile tugged at his serious mouth. "You don't even know what I was going to say."

"Yes, I do." She took his hand, made him sit next to her. "You can't have your freedom, Mitch. I won't let you go."

His jaw dropped before he managed to compose himself. "You think I want my freedom?" He laughed mirthlessly, then rubbed his eyes hard. "Good God, Jussie."

"Isn't that what you were going to say?"

"No, dammit!" He lowered his voice with visible effort and rubbed his eyes again. "I was going to offer you *your* freedom."

"Why would I want that?" she asked very softly.

He dropped his hands from his face and looked at her wearily. "Don't you?"

"No—"

"Don't." His voice came in a tortured whisper now, as if each word were being dragged forcibly from his throat. "Don't make this any harder than it already is. You saw what happened tonight. You saw me hesitate to save you. How could you trust me after that?"

"You can't mean that very first instant when Hopkins appeared." She remembered his shock, how his gun had slipped down to his side. "How could you have known you'd have to save me from a man you've trusted and believed in for two years?"

"I should have." He sounded so disgusted, so weary. "Because I didn't, you were nearly killed right in front of me. Mitzy was hurt."

"Mitch." Her eyes had filled again, with so much love and affection, she thought she might die, in his arms this time, if he would ever wrap them around her. "I love you," she whispered. She smiled through her tears when he flinched. "I love how loyal you are, how much you care about the people you let into your life. It's those very things that had you pausing when you saw Hopkins—your loyalty, your affection. It made me love you even more."

He held himself still.

Very gently, she reached up and took his big strong hands in her much smaller ones. For a minute she stared, fascinated at their difference. Fascinated by the fact that small as she was, huge as *he* was, she could be stronger than he.

"You'll never be able to trust me."

"I trust you with my life," she said simply. "Because you love me."

"I do. More than you'll ever know. God. You're everything to me. He gripped her hands. "You always will be."

Justine pulled one hand free, dipped it down the neck of her shirt, and took off the gold chain. Her two rings dangled as she offered it to him. "Aren't you ever going to ask me to marry you again? I've been waiting and waiting you know."

Mitch smiled through misty green eyes, and took the necklace. His large hands never faltered as he removed the rings from the chain. "I never stopped being married to you in my heart."

"Yeah, well," she said huskily. "You never got to see the best part of my wedding outfit, and believe me it was hot, so I think it's only fair that we do the whole thing over again—"

His mouth cut off her words. They kissed and laughed and cried, and then kissed some more. "I wanted to convince you," Mitch said a minute later when he lifted his head and caught his breath. "I was going to use ice cream."

She laughed, then sobered. "There's us," she whispered. "I don't need anything else. Ever."

Touched, he cupped her face, needing to touch her, see her, feel her. "I've told you only what I wanted, not what I'd like to give to you."

"I don't need anything but you—"

"I give you my life, my heart, my soul." He slipped first her diamond engagement ring on her finger, then the gold band. "Will you be mine?"

Leaning forward, she kissed him, then wrapped her arms around his broad shoulders. "I already am."

EPILOGUE

One year later

If one more overdressed, intoxicated, holly-jolly male patted her cheek, or any other part of her anatomy, Justine Miller Conner was going to scream. In fact, if anything else went wrong today, she'd explode.

Her computer had crashed, her favorite marketing tech had left on maternity leave, and two of her writers had missed their deadlines—her brother included. But her face softened at the thought of Devlin.

Okay, his sports story had taken a backseat to planning his honeymoon, and she understood that. If anyone deserved a terrific honeymoon, it was Dev and Mitzy. Mitzy had been through a hellish year, having to deal first with her father's murder, then with the long, trying therapy to regain the use of her arm. Both had been horribly painful, and Mitzy tended to blame herself for what had happened, but counseling had helped take care of that.

So did the surprising friendship that developed between Justine and Mitzy. Justine might not have easily admitted this, but Mitzy's friendship and easy sisterhood had become very important to her.

Yes, it'd been quite a year, she decided as she watched most of her staff celebrate the holidays.

Devlin had stood by Mitzy's side through all of it, never faltering in his unwavering love, and it made Justine want to burst with pride to watch him. He'd grown up so much. In just a few weeks Devlin and Mitzy would walk down the aisle, with Justine as matron of honor, and she wished them all the happiness they deserved.

A group of noisy carolers brushed past, laughing and singing. Justine smoothed down her dress and wished to be anywhere else. Not that she didn't still love her job and the people she worked with. She did.

In fact, she was working on an investigative series regarding some new rumors about corporate tax fraud, and her source had really come through for her. Mitch had just today insisted on joining forces with her on it, confident that between the two of them, they could blow the lid right off the story.

Secretly, Justine had convinced herself that Mitch stuck close out of that old familiar fear for her safety, but it was so lovely to work with him again on a daily basis, she didn't mind his protective nature.

In fact, she thought with a wicked grin as she remembered the "late" night they'd recently shared in her office, working together had definite advantages.

Of course they had to plan their schedule around their darling daughter, Carly Ann Conner, born nine months to the day after their unforgettable escapade in his convertible the previous winter. Just today, the little munchkin had an important report, then spit up her lunch all over another set of files.

Justine and Mitch alternated caring for the precious mini-tyrant, then swapped their amusing horror stories at night over bath time.

Yes, she had it good.

Around her, the jukebox roared, people chattered, laughed, sang. Everyone made merry but Justine. In spite of everything, she just wanted to be home alone with her gorgeous, sexy husband, with her noisy but oh-so-perfect daughter—yet she'd been forced into this ridiculously festive holiday dress instead.

"Hello there, sweetheart. Miss us?"

At the sound of her husband's low, husky voice, Justine turned with a smile already curving her lips. For a minute she could only stare, love and pride choking her up. Her vision blurred, her voice went husky. "God, there's nothing so attractive as a man with a beautiful baby in his arms."

Mitch wore his tux. Their sweet little girl wore white lace and red ribbons. They had matching, moss-green eyes and crooked grins. And when they both reached for her at the same time, Justine's heart nearly burst.

Santa passed them, ho-ho-ho-ing. Squeals came from every direction as staff members and their families rushed to sit on Santa's lap and put in their wish list.

Mitch cocked a brow. "So, my lovely, pouting wife . . ." He reached over Carly to kiss Justine's full, still-sulking lower lip. "What is it you want from Santa this year?"

"You," she whispered. "All I want is you."

She kissed him back, until he tasted love, happiness,

salty tears, and more warmth and affection than he could have ever hoped for.

"How about *your* wish list?" she asked him.

"I've got everything I could ever want."

Jussie's eyes were still closed as she leaned into him and Carly. Her breath had quickened from the kiss, her cheeks flushed. Mitch thought he'd never seen her look so beautiful. "Absolutely everything."

THE EDITORS'
CORNER

What do you get when you pit the forces of nature against the forces of man? You'll have a chance to find out after reading the four fantastic LOVE-SWEPTs coming your way next month. Two couples face the evil forces in their fellow man while the other two do battle with nature in the form of a snowstorm and a hurricane. The result is four mind-blowing romances that'll leaving you cheering—or crying—at the end!

Loveswept favorite Charlotte Hughes dazzles us with **JUST MARRIED . . . AGAIN**, LOVE-SWEPT #902. Ordered by the family doctor to take time off, Michael Kelly decides to spend Thanksgiving in his mountain cabin, away from the pressures of work. Maddie Kelly wants to spend the holiday in *her* mountain cabin, away from her well-meaning family and friends. Unfortunately, it's the same cabin. Since their separation nearly a year earlier, Maddie and Michael have been avoiding each other. When a sudden case of amnesia and a snowstorm trap them in the mountains, together with two dogs and a stowaway nephew, the couple have no choice but to endure each other's company. As they get to know each other and the unhappy people they've become, they slowly realize that what tore them apart the first time around could be the very thing that binds them together. Charlotte is at her all-time best in this touching novel of love rediscovered.

In the land of **SMOKE AND MIRRORS**, Laura Taylor paves the way for two lost souls in LOVE-SWEPT #903. Anxious to begin a new life, Bailey Kincaid fled from Hollyweird with divorce papers in hand. As co-owner and president of Kincaid Drilling, she's responsible for the safety of her men, and she's determined to make the person who is sabotaging her job site pay. When Patrick Sutton found himself interested in the shy wife of one of his clients, he immediately distanced himself from her. He's stunned to find out the woman who captured his attention years ago is now the strong-willed woman in charge of the construction on his property. Patrick had taught her how it felt to ache for something she could never have, and it hadn't been easy to get him out of her system. He insists that they were never strangers and that they deserve to follow where their hearts seem determined to lead. But can the sorrow that haunted their nights finally be put to rest? Laura Taylor writes a memorable story of fated lovers who discover the great gift of second chances.

In **ONLY YESTERDAY**, LOVESWEPT #904, Peggy Webb teases us with a timeless romance that knows no bounds. A sense of *knowing*, a sense of belonging, and a sense of love have kept Ann Debeau in Fairhope, Alabama. When she haggles with Colt Butler over a charming clock, she's pleasantly surprised at the attraction she feels for the handsome stranger. Sorting through her grandmother's belongings in the attic, Ann Debeau finds a stack of love letters addressed to a man she's never heard of. A hurricane strands her there with the waters swirling ever higher, and Colt comes to her rescue, only to be stuck right alongside her. As they read the letters, a mysterious force whisks them in time to a place where both have been before and into a relationship that was never consummated. In the past, Colt and Ann find a ghost that demands closure and an enduring love that refuses to give up on forever. Peggy Webb challenges us to believe in destiny and reincarnation, in this jewel of a Loveswept.

And in **LOVING LINDSEY**, LOVESWEPT #905, Pat Van Wie introduces neighboring ranchers and one-time best friends Lindsey Baker and Will Claxton. Years ago, a misunderstanding drove Will from Willowbend, Wyoming, but he's always known that one day he would return to the land he loves best. Never one to desert a lady in need, he offers Lindsey help in sorting out the trouble at her ranch. Though he swears he's looking to buy his land back from her fair and square, Lindsey's sure that Will is the one responsible for the "accidents." When one night of promises in the moonlight leads to more than just kisses, the dueling ranchers realize they're not just fighting for her land. In the end, will the face of her betrayer belong to the man she's dreamed of for so long . . . or the man she's trusted for all of her life? Pat Van Wie proves once more that those we love first are so often those we love forever.

Happy reading!

With warmest wishes,

Susann Brailey   *Joy Abella*

Susann Brailey   Joy Abella
Senior Editor   Administrative Editor